CLARA

CLARA

by Luisa Valenzuela
translated by Andrea G. Labinger

Latin American Literary Review Press
Series: Discoveries

The Latin American Literary Review Press publishes Latin American creative writing under the series title *Discoveries*, and critical works under the series title *Explorations*.

Library of Congress Cataloging-in-Publication Data:

Valenzuela, Luisa.
    [Hay que sonreir. English]
    Clara/by Luisa Valenzuela; translated by Andrea G. Labinger.
    p. cm. — (Series Discoveries)
    ISBN 1-891270-09-5 (pbk.)
    I. Labinger, Andrea G.H. Title III. Discoveries
PQ7798.32.A48 H313 1999
863—dc21   99-058225

Latin American Literary Review Press
121 Edgewood Avenue
Pittsburgh, PA 15218

**NATIONAL
ENDOWMENT
FOR THE ARTS**

Acknowledgments

This project is supported in part
by grants from the
National Endowment for the Arts in Washington, D.C.,
a federal agency,
and the
Commonwealth of Pennsylvania
Council on the Arts.

PENNSYLVANIA
COUNCIL
ON THE
ARTS

Table of Contents

PREFACE 11

THE BODY 13

I 15
II 21
III 29
IV 49

TRANSITION 59

I 61
II 67
III 81
IV 87
V 92
VI 96
VII 100
VIII 106
IX 112
X 121

THE HEAD 125

I 126
II 133
III 141
IV 146
V 155

Preface

To slip back into my twenty-one year old skin isn't easy. I must do it, however, in order to try to recapture the moment when I wrote my first novel, which I initially entitled *Clara, cuerpo y cabeza.* Later I opted for *Hay que sonreír*: an imperative.

The young woman who wrote *Clara* was living in Paris at the time with a French husband and an infant daughter. During the sacrosanct siesta hour, while the husband worked and the baby napped, instead of washing dishes or doing some other equally essential chore, she began to write, in amazement and desperation. The amazement came from being able to spill out onto the page something like a mental movie made up of apparently arbitrary scenes which became crucial ten pages later. The young woman, having written a few short stories, was now discovering longer narrative. As for the desperation, perhaps it could have been called nostalgia for a distant, yearned-for Buenos Aires. It felt good to be able to sit down and put it on paper. One question remained: why not describe that luminous, festive world that she missed so much? Her mental rambling through the underworld presented a paradox which the budding writer didn't know how to resolve. She still felt a strong fascination for the old amusement park, Parque Retiro, and those slightly clandestine trips with her inseparable gang to lowlife hangouts like El Avión, a dance hall in La Boca.

All first novels are autobiographical, they used to say in those days. However, in this case she seized the bull by the horns and sketched a biography that was as different from her own as could be. Just like that. Without planning to. Because the idea for a story came to her, with a beginning and an end but nothing in between. And she realized that it had to be a novel, that the central knot had to be a connection of knots and nooses that would grow tighter and tighter until the final dénouement.

That woman who was myself forty years ago finished the first draft thanks to Michel Chodkiewicz, a reader for Editions du Seuil who every so often sent me a brief note requesting thirty or fifty more pages by a certain date. It turned out to be an invaluable incentive. Then came all the rest of it: the upheaval of moving the family back to Argentina, the joy of returning, as well as the problems, the sensation of not knowing how to polish the manuscript. And something else, besides. It seemed to me that the book lacked humor, the worst of all sins. What had I done, writing the pathetic, candid story of a candid prostitute? *Clara* remained in a drawer for a few years. Until one day I dared to reread it, and I laughed and laughed because it struck me as the most quintessentially *porteño* story imaginable, and at that point I was able to polish the manuscript and even won a prize from the Fondo Nacional de las Artes for its publication in 1966.

In 1976 it was published in English, thanks to the good offices of two people at Harcourt Brace Jovanovich: Henry Raymont, who discovered me, and Drenka Willen, who also believed in me. My eternal thanks to both of them.

Now for a confession about the plot:

When I was twenty-one I knew nothing about the open ending as a literary technique, but no doubt that's what I wrote. Each reader has the right to finish the novel as he sees fit, although even today I still believe (as I did yesterday) that Clara doesn't die: there's no more effective weapon than confusion against someone who thinks he's the sole possessor of all truths.

And another confession, this one literary:

I spent my youth close to Borges, and he was very fond of me as well. When *Hay que sonreír* was published, someone or other told him about my novel, and for a long time things weren't the same. Borges said at the time that I was a pornographic writer. It hurt me; it infuriated me. This deliberately naïve story, pornographic? Now I know that Borges was right, as always: it's a simple matter of checking the dictionary: *pornographer*: one who writes about prostitution (*Pequeño Larousse Ilustrado*). A second definition, from Webster's Unabridged, says: from the Greek, *pornógraph(os)*: writer or writing about harlots.

As simple as that. And also, luckily, as complex.

L.V.

The Body

I

*H*ow deadening it is to wait! With her left foot she scratched her right leg, a gesture that meant resignation. Her name was Clara, and she was fed up. Who would ever get the crazy idea to put on new shoes just to wait, and make a date in a place where you can't sit down? And that Victor – he made me show up before eight o'clock to avoid the crowds, and now it's almost eight thirty and no sign of him! I ought to know him by now: he goes around talking about peace, and he sucks in everything he says like it was smoke from an expensive cigarette, but he's got no peace. Because as long as he has someone to impress, he won't even remember our date. And poor Clara, too worn out from struggling against her own defects – she's not about to attack the few virtues he has left at this stage of the game. She was on time, naturally. She'd been waiting for him since before eight, and no doubt he was sitting at the counter in some bar, talking to some stranger and sagely uttering words like ""silence," only to fall silent afterwards and savor the silence he himself had brought on.

In Victor's life, boredom and monotony had nothing to do with each other, and his repertory was repeated so often that, even from a distance, Clara could follow his conversations with his soon-to-be neighbors at the bar:

"Well, sure, you've got to take it with soda," the other guy would conclude when he had grown tired of Victor's long diatribes.

But he wasn't about to let himself be cowed by any irrefutable cliché or lose the opportunity to have the last word:

"Not with soda, my friend; soda makes bubbles. It deceives you and distracts you. Take it from me, life should be drunk with clean, pure water, the kind that quenches your thirst."

Unfortunately, Clara was all too familiar with Victor's _bons mots_, although she never knew exactly when he would decide to dump them on her. At first, of course, she had listened to him attentively, hoping to become his initiate into the secret of harmony and the golden mean, as he called them, but very quickly she discovered that he spoke the same way to everyone and that he had no special mystery to reveal to her; at that point, she chose to wait for him – not too impatiently – while he spewed out his need to be misunderstood on others.

The street lamps in the plaza began to light up one by one, the hands of the clock in the English Tower mercilessly showed eight thirty, and the big neon star of Parque Retiro started blinking on and off above Clara's head, as if it were real. The sky had turned a deep blue, and for a moment she was able to think of the sea and feel happy. That precise moment of happiness can sometimes redeem an entire day, a month, even a year of indifference and impenetrability, because the sea was one of Clara's favorite dreams. The people rushing toward the station through a curtain of humidity lumbered as heavily as underwater creatures, and even though the Southern Cross hadn't yet appeared, she fixed her gaze on the exact spot where it was hiding, and she tried not to move or think so she could discern it sooner.

That's how she waited for everything: with that weariness caused by waiting. She even waited for Victor… without too many expectations, it's true, because for her, everything came too late.

It's never too late for happiness, a friend once said, trying to console her. But the only fragments of that saying that remained in her consciousness were the words *late* and *never*, which got muddled together forever in a single, irredeemable truth. That's how it was with Victor, who remembered things at the wrong time, when they were no longer essential.

She raised her left arm to look at her wrist, but she left off in mid-gesture. Just in time she remembered that she had pawned her wristwatch three days before. It had been a real sacrifice to give it up, but they needed the money, and Victor was such a serious guy that he wouldn't let her work the streets, like before. Streetwalker, as they say… And there was Victor, always going on about how he was a decent man, and a decent man would never allow his wife to be a prostitute.

As if they were married, Clara said to herself but decided to keep quiet because you could never have the last word with him. For that reason, she had decided to pawn the watch, as well as a silver *mate* handed down from her grandfather, rather than get involved in useless arguments. Of course she carefully put away the receipts, waiting for the day when she might redeem her treasures. And in that business of waiting, she was an apt pupil. Taught by Lady Experience herself.

The enormous English Tower, with its brick body and its illuminated sphere on top, would not allow her to forget about time passing. You couldn't even see the squares of grass on the plaza any more, and the streams of water from the slowly-revolving hoses had already been turned off. Naturally, Victor hadn't shown up yet. No doubt, it was his destiny to arrive too late, just like the night she met him. The shell of anguish that had been growing around her little by little for so many years had locked her inside, and no one could pull it off her any more. She wondered whether it wouldn't just be easier to leave everything in the hands of fate and shrug off all her responsibilities, but she realized that her anguish wasn't his fault.

It wasn't that her former line of work had made her unhappy, no. Or that she had liked it, either. She did it without thinking, like when she arrived from Tres Lomas and got off the train at the Once Station. In her hometown she had been told that the prettiest part of the capital was Palermo Park, with its lake, its swans, and such a well-tended rose garden. But when she descended the flight of stairs from the station, she found herself facing a square, uninviting plaza, with a square, uninviting monument, and lots of unfamiliar people scurrying along the wide avenues, breathing fumes from the millions of buses and streetcars (also unfamiliar) that squealed around the corners. She walked around the plaza once, lugging her cardboard suitcase, until she ran into an elderly man with a kind face and decided to ask him how to get to Palermo. The man thought she was talking about Palermo Station and told her to take bus number 268. Because of a simple misunderstanding attributable to her suitcase, Clara arrived at Palermo Station, where there were no trees, let alone lakes with swans, and where the only roses she saw were a few that were wilting in the window of one of those florist shops that smell like cemeteries. But next door to the florist's there was a window with silk and lace blouses and bell-shaped skirts.

Since she had time to kill, she hung around looking in the windows. Her father had told her she was all grown-up now, and she could go look for a good job in the city, and she didn't even have time to object, because her father had locked himself back up in the bedroom where she had caught him with the butcher's wife. What else could she do but take off her apron, put on her coat, and leave the house docilely without waiting for her mother, who would perhaps get back from her long trip to Quemú-Quemú in a few days. She walked about a mile to the station and took the 11:45 train in order to see the park in the city, but once she got there, the blouses tempted her and kept her glued to the shop window.

From far off, a sailor who had been watching her with a glint in his eye waited a long time before deciding to approach her:

"All alone, baby?" and then, "Pretty blouses, aren't they, honey?"

"Uh-huh."

"But you're even prettier."

She laughed. The boy seemed nice, and since he was in the navy, his uniform was blue, not ugly green like the others. For that reason alone, blue versus green, Clara agreed to have a drink with him at the bar across the street. She was hungry, besides, but she didn't know how to go about ordering the sandwich special. She quaffed the martini in a single gulp in order to reach the olive at the bottom, and she sucked insistently on the pit. But such a meager mouthful didn't assuage her hunger, and she was afraid that the rumbling in her stomach would start to grow too loud. She asked a question to conceal the noise:

"Is the sea pretty?"

"Hey, I don't know. I've been in the service for a year already, and we haven't even gotten out of port once. The guys say the ship is such a old tub that it can only float on the river, where the water's all thick and filthy."

He laughed, and Clara could see he had two teeth missing, which detracted somewhat from his charm. Besides, this business about never having seen the sea must be kind of devastating for a sailor. Without feeling guilty, she accepted a second martini, and a third. By then she felt courageous enough to order the special, but he had worked out a better plan:

"How about if we take a little walk to the hotel and go upstairs. They have nice little rooms, pretty and warm…"

Clara's elbow was resting on the table, her head in her hand. Outside, it must have grown cold and dark, and the bar was so lovely, with so many windows and curtains, a little dirty, maybe, but so lovely. She looked at the sailor indifferently. Everything seemed lovely and indifferent at the same time, and she felt like she was floating. She shrugged her shoulders, smiled a little out of the corner of her mouth, thinking she was making a face and answered:

"If you want to…"

The room on the second floor, with its iron bed, was anything but pretty. And it was cold. The man who took them upstairs ran to close the window. "You gotta air 'em out in between customers, right?" and he left them alone.

Clara didn't even notice him undressing her. Once she was in

bed, she tried to ask his name, although there really wasn't much of
him left without his uniform, and his name became garbled in his moans.
He had to get up at 5 AM and return to the ship, but since he was the
great deflowerer, he was so pleased with himself that he left one hundred pesos on the nightstand for Clara and ran downstairs to tell the
others about the great score he'd made in Plaza Italia. Now he was a
real man.

Clara, on the other hand, awoke rather late with a terrible head-
ache and a strange, pasty taste in her mouth. She began to recall what
had happened, but the money she found on the nightstand helped her
overcome her now useless shame. She dressed slowly and, standing
before the mirror, assumed a deliberately vacant expression that might
help her step out of the elevator and walk through the café with dignity. But as she passed the cash register, the boss approached her, and
she lost her composure.

"Miss, you're very wise to honor our humble establishment. Here
you'll find discretion and every comfort you'll need, if you'd care to
return with another acquaintance."

He cleared his throat, straightened his tie, and slyly slipped thirty
pesos into her coat pocket. Terrified, Clara looked around her. There
were hardly any customers at that hour of the morning, and she left
thinking that life in the city wasn't too pleasant after all, but it wasn't
as bad as they had told her, either. And it was so easy... She walked
into another café and ordered hot chocolate with croissants while she
made her calculations and then returned to the shop window where the
blouses were, this time to look at the prices.

She stayed there for a much longer time than it took to determine
that the one hundred thirty pesos she had earned – she hesitated at the
term *earned*, preferring *obtained* – well, anyway, that one hundred
thirty pesos plus the twenty seven she had brought with her from home
wouldn't pay for something that cost the exorbitant sum of one hundred ninety-nine pesos and ninety cents. She stood looking into the
shop window, eyeing the street in the secret hope of seeing the sailor
again, but finally she got bored and began walking towards down-
town, studying all the passing uniforms.

She had forgotten about the shop windows until she came to a
German restaurant adorned with wood, with a sign that said: Inside
Patio. It was already noon, and some hot chocolate with croissants
weren't enough to fill the stomach of a person like her who had such a
physically wearing occupation. Inside, the patio could very well have

been Palermo Park with the lake and the swans they had described to her. She decided to go in.

The patio wasn't so big, but there were little tables with red tablecloths out in the sunshine, and the steak with French fries was almost as delicious as the dessert with cream and *dulce de leche*. She absolutely did not miss Tres Lomas. When she left, she discovered that her capital had been considerably diminished, but she wasn't too worried. She had enough to last till nighttime. Later, she'd see.

II

*T*he Southern Cross appeared at last, staining the sky, and Clara could no longer find an excuse to keep staring upwards, recalling her past. Victor was the only thing missing. Her legs were starting to grow numb, and she was afraid her impatience would win out. She was categorically opposed to any kind of negative emotion, and she never wanted to let herself be carried away by anger or desperation. She began to walk in order to shake off her gloomy thoughts, and she was well rewarded because she found a ledge in the wall where she could sit down, in front of a store that sold regional souvenirs. At least there she could be comfortable.

If only Victor would take a little longer so I can rest and take off that shoe that's been rubbing my heel. Ever since I arrived at the capital, I've been doing too much walking; or rather, ever since my fourth customer, the one with the broad-brimmed hat with no band, that he didn't even take off when he threw himself on the bed. I remember I asked him if we could have a drink before going upstairs, one of those drinks that make you feel indifferent.

"A drink? Fuck that! I pay you to lay down, not to sit at a counter! Or maybe you think my money grows on trees?"

The customer is always right. And since one always has to keep on going, at that moment Clara decided to go cold turkey. She would be led to sacrifice with her mind completely clear, like those cows she had seen being taken to the slaughterhouse, who surely knew they were about to die.

As she might have guessed, the guy didn't waste a single moment worrying about her. He finished his business, leaped out of bed, buttoned up his pants and jammed on his hat, which had fallen off in an involuntary gesture of courtesy.

He shook the lady by the arm: "Get up, numbskull! Time to get out of here!"

"You can go if you like; I'm going to stay and sleep some more."

"You think I'm paying for this room so you can snore in it?"

"Don't worry, it's the same price, regardless," Clara yawned, trying to cover her face with the corner of the pillow.

"Same price, my ass! I'm paying for every minute. Now get up nicely, or I'll…"

The way things were turning out, it was hardly worthwhile for her to protest. She decided to get dressed with deliberate slowness and go downstairs, putting on her best expression of distaste.

When she passed by the counter, the man at the cash register, the one who had given her the thirty pesos and who smiled at her every time he saw her enter the café, took pity on her. Pity coupled with self-interest, because he summoned her into the cloakroom, where with one sorrowful hand he rubbed her cheek while pawing her behind with the other.

"Take this key, honey. Go up to room five and wait for me there. I'll make you feel better."

When Clara got to room five – a room she hadn't occupied before – she imagined it must belong to the boss because it was so luxurious, with a print bedspread and curtains and a wardrobe and everything. She needed to savor that hopeful moment, licking her lips: the boss had sent her up to his own room. Maybe one day the boss would marry her. She sat down on the edge of the bed, opposite the bathroom, to wait for him; she folded her hands in her lap and lowered her eyes.

A few minutes later the man arrived, immediately flicked off the overhead light, and lit the bedside lamp. More intimate that way, he said. Then he lay the lovely Clara down on the bed and disappeared behind the half-open closet door for a long time. Finally he reappeared, completely naked, and Clara lost all hope because he was clammy and white like those creatures she had seen in the fish store that morning and which someone-or-other had called squid. She decided to call him the Squid, and when the man ordered her to place her open palm on his belly, she was surprised it was neither cold nor slimy.

She woke up the next morning. Like a good housewife, she went to open the blinds, and the sudden burst of light brought her back to reality, that is, to disappointment as usual. The boss? What a joke! The man who had slept with her couldn't even be anyone important in the hotel because he didn't live in that elegant room: the wardrobe, which had been left open, was empty, and the few hangers seemed sad not to be bearing the warm weight of clothing.

It's not even worthwhile to waste time dreaming.

No one will ever marry me, ever. If that's what you want, you've got to say no, act shy. And I can't go around doing that any more.

A while later, she heard a gentle knock on the door, and the Squid entered with a large tray, without waiting to be invited in.

"Don Mario's brought his darling some breakfast..."

So, your name is Don Mario. So, now I'm your darling. And you're bringing me breakfast. Not so bad.

She demurely covered her breasts with the sheets and gave him a sweet smile. Don Mario placed the tray on her knees, and she started to drink that warm café au lait that gave her a much more comforting feeling than making love. Naturally, the Squid had to give her a hard time and spoil everything:

"I don't understand how a refined girl like you can go around doing these things."

"What things?"

"These things!" and he pointed to the bed, angrily.

"Out of necessity." And she dipped a croissant in her café au lait.

"Where do you live?"

"Here, for now."

A few little drops of coffee spilled on the chlorine-scented sheet, and Don Mario became alarmed. But it was too serious a moment to worry about trivialities.

"Dear God, woman! I can't have you staying here. Don't you understand? The boss doesn't want to have anything to do with long-terms. He says he's got enough headaches with the hourlies; he needs the business, but not that bad..."

He caressed her naked back with his hand, and she replied, "Don't worry about me, mister. I sleep with men..."

Nevertheless, she didn't like to talk about such things in the light of day. It would be nicer to go to the zoo, or to the movies. Right near the hotel there was a cinema with continuous shows where you could see the same movie three times in a row. Exactly what she needed: that way, there wasn't a single detail left out. The first time she looked at the pictures; the second time she read the subtitles; and the third time she tried to do everything at once and figure out what the story was about. The last time was the most exciting, but she couldn't explain that to the Squid.

Instead, she repeated, "I sleep with men."

"You're such a birdbrain, girl! If I wanted to exploit you, I'd be a millionaire. But I'm not one to take advantage," he sighed. "And besides, these days everything's become so risky. But I'm not going to hurt you, you'll see. I'm going to protect you like a father."

For whatever that's worth! If only you knew about my father…

"Like a father, that's right," Don Mario repeated, getting down to business. "How old are you?"

"Eighteen."

"Good, at least you're not a minor. Though you don't look it… I would've guessed sixteen, at the most… Tell me, how long have you been around here? But you're eighteen, right? A woman already… Imagine, I thought you were just a kid… I even told myself you might be fifteen. What a pity, huh?"

Who on earth can understand these men! First they say one thing, then another! First they tell you it's better you're not a minor, and then they wish you were fifteen!

To make him feel better, she wanted to tell him that up until five days ago she was still what they call a virgin, but go figure out how you can explain such delicate matters.

"Well, don't worry. I'm going to help you, anyway. Got any savings?"

"No."

"You see? You see what I was telling you? You don't know squat about life, girl! You think you can go around like this forever, without thinking of the future, without a roof over your head and not a penny in your pocket? If you're counting on those poor slobs you pick up in Plaza Italia… You see how that guy dumped you last night. Besides, one guy a night is nothing. You've got to pick up two, three, four, how should I know! There are some girls who even find ten. And don't put on that face for me… hey, you'll get used to it. But you need a little place to rest…"

"Look," he added, as though it were a sudden inspiration. "Look, I'm going to make a deal with the boss to rent you a little room at a special price – since we're friends – and in exchange, you'll bring me a lot of clients. Besides, the days you pick up more than three who order drinks, I won't charge you anything. But you don't have to tell them you live here, and that way they can rent another room. Of course, they have to pay you separately. Okay? Don't be a dummy."

Clara nodded, understanding that she was being led down a path she hadn't chosen. Maybe that's how things turned out in life, without taking one's opinion into account. It's probably already been written, as they say.

"You'll see how the room will turn out practically free for you,… so long as you do me a little favor once in a while, of course."

So as not to waste time, he demanded his little favor right away, to seal the pact, as it were. He stretched out in the bed almost without undressing, and Clara did what she could, but the pact remained only half-sealed, and that very morning she discovered that, although any time of day is good for fucking, some men just aren't all that well equipped. It was a relief.

It's too bad about Don Mario; he turned out to be really nice. A squid with a heart of gold. And I'm a woman now, just like he told me that time, but I haven't gotten that far in life. Having someone to wait hours on end for is a change, but it's not exactly a step forward. The best thing is to make them wait for you, like a lady. One day, who knows when my turn will come... For now, the ledge in this wall is comfortable and narrow, and my feet still hurt.

She walked to the corner in order to think about something else, and she heard arrogant steps approaching, the sound of someone wearing boots.

"Excuse me, miss. Your papers, please?"

It was a suave, slightly tough voice, a guy who spoke out of one corner of his mouth. Frightened, Clara turned around suddenly and saw the well-trimmed moustache and the saber hanging from his waist.

"Oh, officer. I don't have my documents... I left them at home."

"Sergeant!" he corrected her, throwing his head back, and Clara laughed in a tiny voice to show him she wasn't afraid of him and that she liked dominant men.

"You left them at home, huh? And exactly what are you doing, walking around here all alone?"

"I'm waiting for my boyfriend, sergeant."

"Mm-hmm... Does he always keep you waiting?"

"Well,... a lot."

"Bullshit, girl. Don't give me that boyfriend crap. You've been sitting here for a long time. If what you're looking for is a pair of pants, come with me – I'm the best thing you'll find in this market-place."

He laughed, revealing a strong row of teeth.

"You're mistaken, sergeant. I'm not what you think. I assure you, I'm waiting for my boyfriend. How insulting!"

Mustn't let a little blond moustache make you forget Don Mario's advice. Rule number one: don't get involved with the cops.

It all began that time when Clara, feeling more securely established in her little room, had brought that young patrolman, really cute, to the hotel café. And in order to prove to him that she was no beginner, she sat down beside him at the table and called the waiter over with a nod of her head. She was a more familiar figure in there than she was out in the streets, and surely the waiter would give her one of his effusive greetings. But, no. Instead, he approached punctiliously, wiping his metal tray with the napkin he always carried under his arm and asked, "What would the lady and gentleman care to order?" The patrolman asked for a beer, and Clara was about to say "the usual for me" when she noticed Don Mario gesturing desperately at her from behind the counter. The patrolman saw Clara furrow her brow, while behind his back, she saw only Don Mario, whose frenetic hands were waving toward the door and then at her as though they held a revolver. At last she understood. She made an effort to smile at her companion and ordered a cola.

"Heavens! It's already seven thirty!" she exclaimed after a while, looking at the wall clock like a perfect actress. "It's much later than I thought. My mother's going to be worried."

She picked up her purse, leaped up, and added with her broadest smile, "It was a pleasure to meet you, officer. Till next time."

If she had been in the theater, she would have received a standing ovation. She was part of the scene now, and so it didn't even make her laugh to disappear while the poor boy, his mouth hanging open, watched her image infinitely repeated in the mirrors of the café.

She wandered through the streets without looking at the men going by. It was Don Mario's fault; after all, that nice little cop was one of the best clients she had ever found. Young, good-looking, the right candidate to help her discover whether all that brouhaha about going to bed with someone wasn't as nasty as it seemed, after all. She remembered Crazy Eulosia, as she was called in Tres Lomas. She really praised that business to high heaven.

She felt sorry for herself, and big tears began to roll down her cheeks. What a shame that a young girl like me has to work all the time without having any fun. That horrible old Squid made me get rid of the poor, cute little patrolman. To hell with you – you'll never get anything out of me.

She returned to the café an hour later and sat down furiously at a table and asked for a double shot of brandy. From his vantage point, Don Mario noticed that she looked sad and came over to console her.

"Know what? It's better not to get mixed up with the police. He might've asked us for some permit we don't have and thrown us all in the clink. Worst of all, you'd be in danger. As far as we're concerned, we could work it all out for a price, but you'd be lost. That's why I told you to leave. I did it for your own good."

For my own good, sure, you jealous old pig.

"You shouldn't get hooked on the first one who comes along. One of these days you'll find a great guy, you'll see. A great guy, solid as a rock, like the other girls say. Come on, let's get you cheered up!"

He made her order another brandy, and on the pretext of accompanying her, climbed up with her to the third floor, where her room was.

"Can I come in?" he asked when they got upstairs, and Clara allowed him in because she was resigned never to having any pleasure anyway.

Don Mario returned to his duty, patiently explaining that she mustn't get involved with the police, gotta watch out for those cops: those uniforms may be real pretty, but they're dangerous. First they take advantage of a woman and then – boom! – they stick her behind bars. All this, he said, only to conclude with: "Whatever path you may follow, discretion is the highest virtue."

Pompous ass!

But poor Clara assimilated the lesson thoroughly and promised never again to let herself be impressed by the double row of silvery buttons or the little stars that indicated five years of active service. But that guy in front of Parque Retiro, my God, he was stickier than gum, and not as tasty either. Although she had to confess, he had a golden saber and shiny boots. But when Clara made a decision, she was as firm as a rock.

"I'm telling you, my boyfriend will be here any minute."

"You can stop pretending, baby. Don't act so high and mighty with me, 'cause I like my women simple."

If only Victor would have the good sense to show up. Waiting isn't so bad when a girl can dig deep into her memories and find something that's been hidden there for years, but with a blue uniform in front of you, a girl can't even think about anything else.

She leaned against the wall, and the rhythms of the Cuban orchestra that was playing on the other side came through in slow vibrations. The sergeant said a few more words to her, but she didn't even hear them because she was trying to watch the hands of the tower clock move. So late already, and Victor still hadn't come, and this other guy here, all wrapped up in his arrogance.

She looked at her nails, pretending to be distracted, and so she didn't see the other woman pass by, almost touching them. But such things didn't escape the sergeant's attention. He studied the swaying of her hips, and he turned on his heels to follow her.

"May I see your documents please, miss?"

Clara felt relieved by his absence, as if the sergeant's solid body had been weighing on her own.

III

Sometimes waiting turns out to be as tiring as working, because your muscles are all tense and twitching. But feeling tense on Victor's account was something Clara couldn't explain to herself very well. They'd been living together for more than three months, enough time to get used to seeing him show up at the most unexpected times. You've got to loosen up, just like in bed, your whole body, starting with your face, so you won't get wrinkles. You mustn't clench your fists or dig your nails into the palms of your hands. You've got to think about something else, something else. But Victor will never surprise me by showing up on time. Not even the first time.

She met him the very night when all her optimistic ideas and good faith had abandoned her. The only pleasure she had left was to console herself with hateful thoughts which felt warm but which also tore her up inside. She felt like striking out with her bare hands, twisting, wrenching, strangling. Before, she had believed in kindness, but now she didn't even have enough strength left to believe: all the despair in her life was concentrated in that desire to destroy, and she affected indifference as she watched the subway trains go by.

He got off one of those trains right in front of her and gazed at her steadily. He stared for a long time at that pale, abandoned woman with those large eyes. She had a kind of distant beauty, he thought, like that antique portrait he had seen in the window of a bookstore. Very straight, long hair, just like that other woman, and so sad. At last, when the station was nearly empty, the man decided to approach her.

He said, "I don't like tunnels, either. Let's go outside and look at the stars."

Clara smiled bitterly. Someone was reaching out a hand to her, and she ought to accept it. It's so difficult to reject an offer of help.

Together, they took the escalator up to the street and found themselves facing an opaque, dirty sky without a single star.

"Orion's Belt should be over there, behind the Coca Cola sign, and the Southern Cross closer to us, near the church tower," Clara said to him so that he wouldn't be disappointed in his effort to show her the stars. But he wasn't listening to her.

"I'm Victor. And you?"

"Clara."

"Pretty name. Transparent, like peace. Naturally, you couldn't have any other name. That's why I noticed you. I felt compelled to get you out of there. I hate closed-in spaces and crowds and noise. You hate them too, of course. What were you doing, then, lost in the subway? You weren't even looking at the pictures on the walls…"

But he didn't give her time to answer: "Life should be an open space where everything is clear, Clara. Clara, clarity, clear as water, without chlorine."

The phrase struck him as perfect, and he fell silent, savoring it. Clara had the impression he was waiting for her approval, and she tried to explain her thoughts to him.

"I don't understand anything about life, but I think…"

He took her hand and said "Shhh" without letting her finish.

"Don't talk," he added. "The moment is too delicate, too perfect to break it with a sound," and he stood there sniffing the air, as if to breathe in the moment.

They had hardly even become acquainted, and Clara already understood that it wasn't worth the effort to open her mouth with him. The idea of not being able to speak didn't bother her too much because nothing could prevent her from sustaining an internal dialogue, silent but vehement. That same night, sitting on the steps of the new church, they decided Clara would move in with Victor for a while since she had no place else to go.

The apartment, if you could have called it that, was tiny and old, but there was a tree that nearly poked in through the window, and Victor proudly showed her the bedroom set that he had just bought as if he'd had a premonition. The enormous wardrobe, the enormous bed, the two nightstands and a chair occupied and filled the single room. There was nothing in the hall yet, which was a piece of luck, Clara told herself, because there was no room for anything else. Just a mirror, maybe, and a coat rack. The kitchen was long and narrow and did double duty as a dining room. Victor said he would paint it green to keep the flies away. She looked at him admiringly.

"You're rich, then, with new furniture and all?"

"Well,… I have a few little savings. Besides, I'm planning to sell this old radio and buy a new one, you know? One of those little ones with a golden dial."

Clara set herself up in her new home, happy to have a man who gave her his socks to darn and shirts to wash. At least that way she could say she was a real housewife, not a tumbleweed like before. She also had to wash the dishes and the new pots Victor brought her one afternoon because he was tired of eating ham and cheese sandwiches. Clara scrubbed and cleaned without saying a word because he didn't tolerate back talk, and she had lost the use of her voice, although she still operated her imagination skillfully. Her favorite mental dialogue concerned marriage: she had perfected it and was convinced of its indisputable realism, but after a while there were no winners or losers in that debate, since she wasn't at all sure she felt like marrying Victor. On the days when she had nothing to do, she stretched the dialogue out eternally; on the other hand, when she was tired, she condensed it into a few words, to the point where she concluded that it wasn't worthwhile to get married or have children, because, as Victor said, that just complicates things…

Victor had such devastating arguments that it was easier to concede to him, even in her thoughts. Besides, the poor guy tried to be kind to Clara, so she couldn't deny the fact that he was good-hearted. When things were going smoothly, he called her Clarita and took her out walking. But whenever some problem came along, he said it was her fault because she didn't know how to manage a household, and then he would call her "my wife." That's when Clara decided it was much better that they hadn't married, even though it meant giving up the idea of having children. But things went well in general, and Clara knew how to argue with the butcher to get cheaper cuts of meat that would stretch farther, and Victor appreciated her stews. Sometimes, it was true, she dreamed about the blouses and necklaces she had once had, and when she felt really desperate, she would hop over to Plaza Italia – which was quite nearby – although she carefully avoided the area where Don Mario's hotel stood. But her domestic vocation finally won out, and instead of buying the lace slip she was longing for, she came back home with a chicken and a nice bottle of wine. And since the way to a man's heart is through his stomach, Victor never bothered to suspect where those delicacies might have come from.

But the day arrived when Victor confessed that his savings were all gone and that lately he hadn't sold even a single refrigerator.

Clara told him it didn't matter, she could find some customers and – problem solved! But he became enraged.

"Are you crazy? I'm not about to exploit you like that! Do you think I'm so worthless? How can you imagine I'd send you back to that muck I pulled you out of!"

He remained silent for a while, just thinking, and when his rage had simmered down, he added: "Look, Clarita, the best thing we can do is join forces to get over this rough spot. Everything will turn out fine soon enough, you'll see... I'm going to pawn my cufflinks and my tie pin with the pearl. The new radio, too, if you think we should, though I don't think it's really necessary. And you, well,... couldn't you contribute something?"

"Yes," she sighed, and she went to look for her grandfather's silver *mate*, which was in its box. Later, making a great effort, she removed her wristwatch and handed it to Victor without looking at him.

Her grandfather's *mate* didn't matter so much to her. All it did was remind her of her fifteenth birthday, a day which was just as boring as all the rest. But the watch was as much a part of her as her feet or her mouth. It was her trophy; she had earned it in an act of bravery she could never again repeat, and one of her greatest pleasures was to watch the little gears spin while she assured herself that she had managed to escape from a machine just as devilish as that one, and without too many scratches. Of course, luck had been on her side.

Don Mario had always repeated to her, with that characteristic tone he used when he wanted to protect her from the evils of the outside world: "Never go after men in cars... Cars are nice, sure, and men with gold chains are very attractive, but they're the worst ones. God knows where they'll want to take you and what things they'll want to do to you. Your profession isn't such an easy one, y'know? And when some pimp comes along who tries to suck the lifeblood out of you, don't come around sniveling to me, because I'm warning you: forget about cars and fat cats."

Clara had resolved to follow Don Mario's sage advice to the letter. Being a beginner is always tough, and it's good to have someone to guide your steps, but that business about cars stuck in her craw. She wanted to get ahead, and she knew that between a man with a car and another one on foot, there was an enormous difference in economic position. And a different social position. Besides, she wanted to go to the sea, and to do that, you'd need a car with soft seats to sink into and get yourself ready to face the blue, foamy waters. You can't get to the sea straight off a train crowded with fat women and belching men.

But she had never spoken of the sea to Don Mario; she liked to keep a few secrets to muse on in the solitude of her attic room, at the window with no view, just a black roof, dirtied by long-vanished pigeons. Sometimes she imagined the pigeons were still there, hiding, about to turn into seagulls who would come to eat from her hand, and every morning she threw down crumbs, just in case.

Don Mario had also advised her not to get involved with the hotel staff. "They're just a bunch of pathetic losers," he told her, "and you're with the manager. That gives you status. You have to demand dignity in life, my child."

Then he would smile, standing stock-still with pleasure, and she would take advantage of those moments when their bodies weren't touching to close her eyes and imagine that the man at her side wasn't Don Mario, but Carlos, one of the waiters on the afternoon shift at the bar.

Along with the sea, Carlos was one of Clara's illusions. He was tall, with sleek, dark hair, and when you looked at him up close you could see that he had little golden flecks in his eyes. Sometimes Clara ordered him to bring tea and cookies up to her room at five o'clock, the elegant hour, but he had time only to wish her a good afternoon and leave the tray on the night stand. She always told herself that the next time she'd let him in with her robe open a bit, but she couldn't bring herself to do it because Carlos was shy, and she didn't want to make a bad impression on him. And it was for that reason she didn't go out to work until after nine PM, when he had already left.

One afternoon, however, when remaining indoors seemed more oppressive than usual, she went downstairs before eight, carefully made up. She had put on a lavender dress, even though it was too low-cut for those chilly October nights. But if she'd felt too enclosed in her little room, she didn't know what to do in the street. She stood in front of the café window, watching the neon lights change color, and just as she was starting to wish he would notice her and come to her rescue, she heard a voice that tickled the hairs on the nape of her neck.

"Are you waiting for someone, Señorita Clara?"

Startled, she turned suddenly, stammering, "Oh! No, no."

"Am I disturbing you? Are you busy?"

"No!"

Now that she was facing him at last, she didn't know what to say. She ventured a phrase: "The night is so lovely."

"A beautiful night. A night to enjoy. Put ambition aside. Since neither one of us has anything to do, we could have a drink together. What do you think?"

Clara looked at him as if she were dreaming and answered him with a tiny voice: "Yes,..." and she started to walk into the bar.

"No, not here, Clara. May I call you by your first name? Let's find a change of atmosphere. I know a place in the rose garden, facing the lake. We could take a few turns around the dance floor."

"I'm a terrible dancer."

"That doesn't matter. There's so little light – no one will see us."

They looked at each other and laughed. It was the first time Clara had ever laughed at the same time as a man. In general, she usually laughed before, if she was making fun of him, or after, if he said something funny and she forced herself to laugh, to make a good impression. But now she was laughing together with Carlos, and she said, without measuring her words very carefully:

"Let's go to the place by the lake. If no one else sees us, we can have a good time."

He took her arm firmly, and they left the busy street for another, darker one. They walked along silently, and Clara didn't think about anything because Carlos was holding her arm, and she was afraid to break the spell. They didn't exchange another word until Carlos suggested:

"We could call each other *tú*; after all, we've known each other for several months now."

"True."

Nevertheless, neither one spoke again as they advanced into the darkness, while the boulevard lights behind them turned into tiny dots. They didn't hurry. Their steps marked the exact rhythm of a couple. People inside their houses would have remarked, "There goes a man," even though it was a couple passing. Soon Carlos released her arm and draped his own around her shoulders. Clara stood rigidly, without knowing what to do with her arms hanging alongside her body. When they had crossed a street, Carlos stopped her beneath the yellow stain streaming from a street lamp.

"You're too lovely," he said to her, and they continued walking.

Clara trembled a bit, and he pressed her against his chest. "Are you cold?" he asked her, but she shook her head, resting it against his shoulder, and they continued walking.

He raised his free hand, at first caressing her forehead, and then he took one of her hands which was dangling without knowing where to come to rest.

Clara looked at him and asked, "Is that place far away?" because she never wanted to get there, in spite of the lake and the swans.

"You're tired. Let's sit down for a while," he replied, resting on a low wall that faced a garden fragrant with night-blooming flowers. Clara wanted to tell him no, I'm not tired, but Carlos effortlessly drew her towards him and seated her on his knees. She lowered her head, fearful that the emotions hammering against her temples would escape, and he took that opportunity to kiss her hair right at the nape of her neck. Then Clara raised her eyes and discovered the little golden flecks in his eyes, like stars. The little flecks grew closer, and Clara felt herself carried away by a whirlwind as she felt that other warm mouth devouring her own.

Carlos had to make a tremendous effort to wrench himself from the spot, but he stood up and once again put his arm around her shoulder as they moved along. As they walked, he whispered words she couldn't hear but felt were charged with magic.

Lights from another boulevard blinded them. It was an avenue Clara had never seen before, without streetcars or buses, just cars whizzing by, defying the wind. Clara allowed Carlos to worry about choosing the right moment to cross and allowed herself to be carried along, her eyes closed, enjoying the sensation of being protected.

Before them were the woods, barely illuminated by slender lanterns, and beyond, the dense darkness of the foliage which not even the moonbeams could penetrate.

Carlos guided her to the darkest corner of the park, where the shadows of the tree trunks were outlined. He removed his jacket and lay it there, beneath the huge eucalyptus, and on top of the jacket he placed Clara, and then he himself stretched out, on top of the soft form of the woman.

Clara was afraid for what she was, helpless in the face of passion, and for what she was not, for what she had unthinkingly abandoned when she arrived in the city. A single moment of fear, just the time it took for him to separate from her, and then that long emptiness, so filled with man and earth, a step closer to God, and finally, after so many attempts, happiness.

Back at the hotel, Clara wished she could have remained like that forever, with the sensation of Carlos's body floating above hers. She stepped up to the bar and ordered a brandy, smiling beatifically, and she looked at Don Mario without seeing him.

Don Mario, from his perch, studied her, astonished, and called her over before she had finished her drink.

"Clarita, my child, you look strange. You've obviously been out drinking, and you're not used to it. The best thing to do would be to go up to your room and go to bed. Tomorrow morning I'll bring you a nice cup of coffee and some aspirin, and you'll see how much better you'll feel."

Don Mario fulfilled his promise and brought her the aspirin, but Clara had never felt better than she did that morning. She was radiant. Until the avuncular Don Mario broke the spell into a million pieces.

"How many times have I told you not to go out with the hotel staff! Last night around ten, the wife of Carlos Álvarez, the waiter, showed up completely out of her mind, looking for her husband. And Pichi told her he had seen him go out with you. You can imagine the scandal! I was the one to get the brunt of all the shouting, and on top of everything else, we're now short one waiter, because that shrew won't let him come back here even by accident!"

A few words, but they carried the taste of death, because Carlos had gone away forever. Clara rested her head on the pillow and swallowed her coffee and aspirin, in spite of everything, trying to understand why every moment of happiness had to be paid for in blood, without even having time to enjoy it.

Now, with Victor, at least she lived calmly; she wasn't overly happy, and therefore she wasn't afraid that the implacable judges who rule over our lives would try to collect their dues for these tedious days. At the most, they exacted their penance from her by making her wait – not too impatiently – opposite an enormous clock that emphasized the passing hours. It wasn't anything like the time she had waited for Carlos, for three days and three nights, without eating, sleeping, or going out, in order not to be distracted in her waiting.

He deceived me; he never told me he was married, she told herself by way of consolation. But later, her hopes of seeing him again returned, and she admonished herself: I tricked him, too; I never told him how I earn my living. It's all my fault. Yes, he'll come back. The problem is that his wife is a monster who keeps him locked up, but he'll escape. Which doesn't change the fact that he deceived me. At least I didn't betray anybody. I didn't know he has a wife, maybe even kids.

In spite of everything she waited for him steadfastly for three days and three nights, but Carlos never reappeared. The last night, as they were putting the chairs up on the tables to wash the floor, Don Mario took her arm and said to her:

"Come to bed; you could really use it."

Clara followed him, and he behaved very properly in the elevator, without even fondling her between floors, as was his habit. When they arrived at the room, he made her sit down on the bed beside him and said reproachfully:

"You wouldn't obey me, and now you see what's happened to you. I told you not to go out with that waiter, and you disobeyed me. He's the type of guy who hoodwinks women and then disappears forever; I know the type very well. *Now* you won't disobey old Mario again, huh? I told you you've got to be discreet."

He helped undress her and put her to bed. Then he turned off the light and remained sitting in the chair, at her side, despite his desire to go to bed with her, because he knew what Clara needed was to sleep and forget.

Discretion and obedience, Clara said to herself before she fell asleep, lots of discretion and obedience, but if it weren't for you, Carlos would still be here, and I could see him all I wanted.

She slept until the next afternoon, when she was awakened by a tray of hot chocolate and a ham sandwich, courtesy of Don Mario.

She went downstairs an hour later, and walking through the bar, she realized she couldn't go on living there as long as Carlos's memory still floated among the mirrors. Her insides ached with despair, and she left determined to break away and find a man with a car who could take her to the sea.

At first she began to scrutinize the long automobiles that passed by, the ones with two or three different colors and tail fins, but she realized that most of them were driven by uniformed chauffeurs, and she was well aware that any important man could never reveal to a subordinate that he needed a hooker. He'd have to pretend he could have all the ladies he wanted just by crooking his little finger. Of course, ladies at times could play hard-to-get, and sometimes they could be too easy, and in either case they're too expensive and full of airs. That's why gentlemen should sometimes seek out loose women with fixed rates, but never in front of others, least of all in front of their own chauffeurs.

Clara continued waiting for an automobile, however, and she even turned down a blond sailor who was the best goods available in

Plaza Italia. She bent down to smile at all the men driving by, but they were all in too much of a hurry to notice her, until finally a car braked to a halt right next to her. She hadn't smiled at that one because it looked like a pretty old model, but the driver said "hop in" with such authority that Clara obeyed.

As she got in, she noticed that the seats weren't altogether uncomfortable and that she might be able to get to the sea if the engine didn't quit first. She even thought the front seat might recline into a bed, like in that drawing she had seen on the back cover of a magazine condemned as unequivocally immoral by the Catholic Action chapter in her town. It was ridiculous: a thing can't be moral or immoral. Poor little car in the magazine, criticized by everyone. But she hadn't had the courage to defend it, although the following Sunday, she went to confession because of her evil thoughts, and the priest admonished her:

"My child, evil thoughts are like flies: a single one is nothing, but soon it attracts others, and they pile up in a great, rotten mess. Pray three Hail Mary's and three Our Father's."

Clara tried to think about other evil thoughts she had had before that one; she couldn't come up with any. Only just now, when she wished the car could turn into a bed to carry her to the sea. Well, then, she concluded, if there weren't any evil thoughts, she couldn't be rotten. The idea didn't displease her, and she decided to smile when she saw the man in the car eyeing her strangely.

She tousled her hair and said to him: "Let's go to the Almafuerte Bar. It's really nice there."

Bad habit – if I go there, I'll start to think of Carlos again, and I'll never persuade this guy to take me far away.

The man seemed to read her thoughts, because he said, "What? You think I'm a taxi to take you wherever you please?"

Clara stopped stretching herself coquettishly and stared at him wide-eyed.

The stranger lit a cigarette and moved the lighter very close to her face to look at her.

"Are you supposed to go there?"

"No, I'm not supposed to..."

"Who's in charge of you, huh? Because this isn't the first time I've seen you prancing around here with that innocent little look of yours..."

"Nobody's in charge of me."

At that moment Clara thought about sighing – it would be elegant and sad at the same time – but he didn't give her enough time, and he pulled away immediately, saying, "Well, then, let's go where *I* want to go."

The traffic cop put his whistle in his mouth, but by the time he tried to blow it, they were already far away. A few blocks farther down, they had to brake to let a truck go by, and the man asked her, "What's your name?"

"Clara."

"For your information, my name's Toño Cruz. My buddies call me Cruz Diablo."

Clara never found out that this was only half true: his buddies in the first grade had called him Cruz Diablo; later the nickname was forgotten. The other clerks at the bank where he worked treated him with some respect, since he had been with the company for fifteen years. But he repeated, "Cruz Diablo, ha-ha," and patted her on the back.

He started driving again, flooring the gas pedal furiously until they pulled up opposite an austere building with a brown marble façade. The car edged forward towards a closed garage door which opened automatically, letting them in. When Clara turned around to see how the mechanism worked, the door had already closed behind them, plunging them into darkness. A shadow of a man approached them with such a servile demeanor that Clara didn't have to be urged to get out of the car and follow Toño and the man through the shadowy, carpeted corridors.

When the overhead light in the room was turned on, Clara realized that Toño Cruz was much shorter than she had imagined, and his hair was streaked with gray. He had a small head and a pointy face, but Clara reminded herself that a perfect whore shouldn't concern herself with her customers' physical appearance. He was examining her at the same time, which wasn't a problem because a customer doesn't have any reason to be perfect and is allowed to waste time with such foolishness; after all, he's the one who pays.

When he had finished studying her from a distance, he drew closer in order to touch her, clicking his tongue.

"All right, get undressed. Now we're going to try you out."

Clara meekly undressed and started to turn out the light, but he said, "Leave that alone," and she approached him very slowly, like a cat, rubbing up against his body because she was cold.

When they were done, Clara concluded that Toño had enjoyed

her cat act because later on he had tried to do it for her, although he remained distant and abstracted. She decided to play kitten for all her customers so they'd be less rough and give some thought to her feelings: Musn't think about Carlos; mustn't think about Carlos, she told herself, and the phrase was just beginning to lull her to sleep when she heard a sudden rumbling noise.

"What's that?" she asked, startled.

"It's nothing, woman… just the siren of some ship."

Clara sat up in bed and felt her temples throbbing.

"We're at the sea, then, we're at the sea!"

She knew quite well that it took at least five hours of traveling to reach the sea, but they had driven so fast… A boy from her hometown who had studied in Buenos Aires for three years had once explained to her that if you go very fast, time ceases to exist. She hadn't understood him, and she had felt afraid, and ever since that time she had refused to see him again, even though he had confessed that he wanted to marry her. That made her even more afraid; surely his head would have filled up with strange ideas, and he'd have abused and abandoned her. But now everything was different: now nobody could abuse her, and the poor guy's ideas seemed entirely clear to her. They had driven so fast that they'd left time behind and had reached the sea.

But Toño, Cruz Diablo, soon snatched her from her comfortable illusions.

"What the fuck sea are you talking about, you stupid hick? We're near the port. Haven't you ever been to the port?"

"No."

"What about the river? Río de la Plata?"

"Uh-uh."

"And this building?"

"Mmm… no."

"What exactly *do* you know, anyway?"

"Well,… not a lot."

Toño Cruz decided to play his best hand. "Well, then, you've got no choice but to come with me. I'm going to teach you everything you need to know."

"Seriously? But I live in a hotel."

"All alone, right? Then what the hell does it matter? You'll move into my place. A fancy apartment house on Junín Street. It's full of businesses. Do you know the one I'm talking about?"

"And leave my job?"

"Your job? You're not a maid or anything like that, right?"

"Oh, no. *This* is my job."

"Hah! What a laugh! That's not a job; it's a vocation. Don't even think of giving it up. You'll be much better off with me. I'll hang around with you when you're resting. I'll organize things for you real good, and you'll even be able to save up and everything. What do you think?"

Clara thought about Don Mario, poor guy, and his advice. She also thought about the hotel and the bar, where Carlos no longer worked. She felt an urgent need for change, and she asked him, "Will you take me to the sea?"

"Why not, if you behave yourself, maybe for your vacation..."

"And what should I tell the people at my hotel?"

"There's no reason for you to tell them anything. You'll go pick up your things early in the morning while I wait for you in the car. Do you have a lot of stuff?"

"Kind of, but I don't have a suitcase to put it in."

At that moment it occurred to her that a suitcase was an essential part of life, and she had thrown away the one she'd brought from Tres Lomas, because it was falling apart. Later, she had bought some blouses and skirts and two dresses, but not a new suitcase. "I have very little sense of progress," she laughed, thinking that, when she left the hotel, she'd also leave all her sad memories behind and take a step forward.

She took a step, true, but it was sort of sideways, insignificant. She was neither better nor worse off than before. Don Mario's hurt feelings had pained her when he saw her leaving with an enormous package, and said,

"So you're leaving, just like that. That's what I figured; I couldn't hold onto you forever. I'm an idiot."

And then his self-directed insult annoyed him, and he began to shout at her as she walked through the bar without daring to look at him, "Go ahead, just go ahead! If you'd rather live with a pimp, what do I care! But don't even think of showing your face around here anymore. I never want to see you again!"

Clara felt like slamming the door in his face, but it was a revolving glass door which, instead of making noise, gently swayed back and forth, disfiguring Don Mario's fat body which was gesticulating between the tables of the empty bar, unable to stop her.

Toño's apartment was on the ground floor, facing the courtyard.

It was large, and it had its own little patio, which wasn't very useful because the sun never reached it, and the neighbors used to throw their garbage out through the windows. Besides, the soot that fell like black rain stuck to the freshly-washed clothes that Clara began to hang out to dry a few days after she arrived.

Nevertheless, her enthusiasm during those first few days made up for all the previous sacrifices she had endured. Upon arriving there, Clara discovered some plants in the entry hall: they had long, hard green leaves, but they symbolized life amid so much darkness. After a few days, she realized they didn't even require watering, as evidenced by the doorman's indifference to them, and they were covered with dust. But whenever she returned home late at night and no one could see her, she watered them with the big glass in which they kept their toothbrushes.

Except for a few details, Clara worked as before, acquiring quite an ability to attract customers and dispatch them as quickly as possible. From time to time, she missed her former neighborhood in Plaza Italia, where there were so many young men and soldiers, and sometimes she allowed herself the luxury of thinking nostalgically about Carlos, although the hotel she frequented most was small and ugly, not like Don Mario's.

She recalled the time a group of tourists had arrived from the provinces, such happy people, singing and playing the guitar; sometimes she heard them because their rooms were right below hers. But what she missed most was Don Mario's relieved smile whenever she returned with a man who looked too old or ugly. It was because of that, her need to find another smile that would give her the courage to go on, that one day she said to Toño:

"Don't you think it would be better if I brought my customers here? It would be much more elegant, and we could charge them for the hotel room and everything."

Toño looked at her, astonished, and studied her for a while before replying:

"You're crazy as a loon, woman! What would the neighbors think, and the doorman and his wife and children! Besides, you know perfectly well that the woman in 1C is a real lady, and she'd be spooked to live just one floor away from a hooker. And she's a friend of the landlord, too. She might tell him and get us thrown out. You should never offend a lady's sensibilities."

And so she wouldn't offend anyone's sensibilities, Clara kept on going to that seedy hotel and handing over all the money she earned to Toño. At first he had asked her for rent money, later for money to pay the gas bill, and then, money for food.

Finally one day Clara got angry: "With what I give you, you'd could pay for food, rent, gas, electricity, hot water, and even buy a car for all the neighbors!"

But he wasn't about to let himself be intimidated: "I knew you were an ingrate. Didn't I give you status? Didn't I give you a home? But no, you had to let loose with one of your insults, didn't you? For your information, I'm not robbing you. I'm investing your money in stocks, so it'll grow, and one day you could be rich. If I let you do whatever you feel like doing, you'd buy yourself a thousand worthless pieces of junk without thinking of saving. So, you see, I do your thinking for you: with those stocks, you'll have a handsome pension in your old age. You know damn well that a whore can't keep on working forever. After a while her body wears out, and no one wants her any more."

She couldn't have cared less about the stocks, but that business about a worn-out body was something she kept mulling over. When she had finished with her last customer of the evening, she rented the hotel's deluxe room for herself, and she contemplated her reflection in the ceiling mirror (the only mirror in the room) for a long time. It wasn't very easy to see herself lying down, but at least she could tell that it would still be quite a while before her body wore out. She cheered up and decided to retire from the profession before her body deteriorated, thanks to Toño's stocks.

She returned to work with renewed enthusiasm and hope, until Toño informed her that he had quit his job at the bank. Nonetheless, Clara watched him leave every morning, clean shaven and wearing a tie. She was too tired to get up and follow him, and she didn't even have strength enough to ask him where he was going. Finally, one day he showed up with a pair of gold cufflinks adorned with large topaz stones. At that point, Clara, in spite of having worked all night long and feeling more like sleeping than fighting, summoned up her courage and shouted at him:

"I'm all fed up with working for you! I can't even buy myself a decent pair of earrings, and you go around dressed like Mr. Moneybags at my expense! It's all over! Gimme my stocks because I'm taking off right now. You hear me? I'm out of here!"

Toño stuck his chest out, standing on tiptoe to reply:

"Fine, beat it, go on, and I'll go to the police station and report you. Got your papers in order, by any chance? You think you have the right to work like you do? You won't get rid of me so easy…"

Clara closed her eyes, and as everything spun around her, she understood that it wasn't the ideal moment to stand up to him, but at least she would extract a promise:

"Okay, I'll keep working for you if you take me to the beach for a few days."

"The beach? What goddamn beach? Gas is very expensive, and I'm not in the mood for jokes."

Two big tears rolled from her eyes, and Toño felt happy, telling himself that all you had to do with women was treat them badly, and that from now on he could do whatever he wanted to with her because he was the one who ran the show. From that day on, he began to shout at Clara and abuse her.

"Two hundred pesos! Two hundred pesos! You've been out for twelve hours, and you only bring me two hundred pesos! You're a piece of shit. What do you expect me to do with your miserable two hundred pesos, tell me. I need money! Money!"

Or:

"What do you mean by coming back so early? You think you've finished your shift? Well, let me tell you something, you haven't finished anything. Rain's no reason to come back after only two customers. Or is Madame so high and mighty that she'd like to rest?"

He shouted so loudly and echoed so resoundingly that Clara began to suspect he was hollow inside, like a bass drum. One day she left earlier than usual and returned later. As she undressed in the dark, Toño thought he saw a suspicious gleam on her wrist.

"What's that you've got there?" he shouted, turning on the bed lamp.

"A wristwatch."

"Oh, yeah? Now you go around buying gold jewelry without my permission, hey? But you'll see what I'm gonna do…"

The watch was made of heavy gold, with a fifteen-jewel mechanism and a one-year guarantee. Clara smiled with satisfaction, which so infuriated Toño that he leaped up and slapped her.

Clara stared at him, wide-eyed, not even managing to bring her hand to her stinging cheek.

Pleased with her reaction, Toño settled back into the bed, saying to himself, I understand women like the back of my hand. This will calm her down for a while. He added aloud:

"Tomorrow we'll straighten out this craziness of yours. You'll tell me where you bought that ridiculous watch, and I'll go exchange it for something I can use."

Clara didn't have the slightest intention of exchanging it, so when Toño returned the next day after paying his customary visit to the lady in 1C, the landlord's friend, he discovered that Clara had vanished forever, taking all her clothing and even a first-rate fake crocodile suitcase of his. Alarmed, Toño ran to the wardrobe to rummage through his winter underwear. Too late – the 1300 pesos he had hidden there awaiting the arrival of the smuggler who would bring him the French perfume for the lady in 1C were missing too.

A place for everything, and everything in its place, as that guy who grabbed her away from Toño and tried to put her in a whorehouse said. And now here was poor Clara, waiting by the side entrance of Parque Retiro, as out of place as an animal in the zoo, or a sailor without a ship, trying to keep his balance, or a mouse in a rainstorm. Whereas other people were where they rightfully belonged, hurrying toward the train station to catch the train that would keep on running for them, without interrupting its single-minded movement. And those who had time were in the waiting room, which, as its name suggests, is made for waiting. Only she was where she didn't belong, standing in a place which everyone passed through and where no one would ever think of stopping. There she was, looking at a brick tower that wouldn't let her forget the minutes passing within the total uselessness of time.

Let's listen to time passing, she used to say to the daughter of her mother's employers, during a long summer *siesta*. But that was a country town, where lost hours didn't matter, and she would enclose herself in the dark living room with the boss lady's daughter, where they would lie under the table and look at the slip-covered furniture and listen to the tick-tock of the grandfather clock. In those days time was a gentleman with a cane and a wooden leg who walked around, quietly growing old.

But now there was no wooden-legged gentleman across from the huge gray train station, just unassailable, exasperating adult time, ticking by while Clara waited for a man with two flesh-and-blood legs who should be arriving any moment now.

People passing by looked at her askance, disapproving of her precisely because they knew she was waiting for someone else. You can wait hours for a bus or a train without arousing anyone's suspicions; the person next to you might even say in a complaining tone, What a nuisance! That streetcar's never going to come! The bus runs much more often, you know? But I can only take the number 31. You think they might be on strike?

If you're friendly and well-informed, you answer, no, they're not on strike, because we would've seen it in the paper. But when it comes, it'll be so full we won't even be able to get on..."

And everyone's so cheerful, because waiting in line lends a certain dignity to the wait. People going by say, What a bother! Public transportation gets worse all the time. You've really got to have patience! And it's just fine.

But when a woman waits alone on a street corner, instead of feeling sorry for her, guys shout:

"Hey, baby, can't you see the guy's left you flat? You've been dumped, sugar..."

Twenty to nine already, and the hands of the clock keep moving forward without worrying about me. Although it's true that most words are chameleons, changing their meaning according to the people who use them, and most truths are too sharp to let themselves be seized by the scruff of the neck. Time is precisely one of those ideas that aren't very clear. I didn't have any problems with Toño, it's true; he let me come and go whenever I pleased. As long as I gave him the money, of course: snap, snap – nice, fresh bills in ready cash. Just one more way to buy time and be able to use it to your liking.

Until she decided to by herself some real time, in a palpable way, in the form of a wristwatch.

After leaving Toño, her great experiment with time ended up costing her dearly. She only managed to set the clock back forty-eight hours to delay her birthday. She wandered up and down the streets; she went into cafés; she peered into shop windows; and when her conscience told her it was time to do something, she consulted her watch and told it no, it's just four-ten. Soon she got bored saying it was four-ten. She wound the watch a little, letting it go for an hour and a quarter, but since it infuriated her to see it advancing so quickly, every so often she systematically turned the hands back a half hour.

Lavalle Street delighted her; people were rushing around, and there were thousands of cinemas. She wanted to rush a bit, too, but the marquees of the cinemas magnetized her, and she crossed from one sidewalk to the other to see the posters. From time to time, some man would approach her and ask "All alone?" in a confidential tone. She was pleasant to all of them, replying no, she had a husband and children, that she liked to go for walks but she had to get back home early. It wasn't the right time to get mad and say I'm not that kind of girl.

By one-fourteen it was already nine thirty, and although Clara repeated to herself that night and day were just heaven's way of playing coy, she began to feel hungry, and she went into a small snack bar along the way. Later she decided she wanted to sleep, and fulfilled her dream of the hotel with its own revolving door.

When she went to bed, she thought that this business of turning nineteen already was painful. Nineteen was an adult age and she ought to start thinking about responsibility. Even though she had seen the date May 22 clearly stamped in the almanac in the entryway, she promised herself she'd never reach nineteen, and thanks to her little watch, May 23 would never arrive.

She slept as long as she could, ate all she wanted, and even saw the same film three times in a cinema that didn't run continuous shows, one of those where you had to go out and pay so you could come in again. But she was able to recapture only two days in her fight against growing old. The 1300 pesos that had been reserved to buy French perfume refused to elude their destiny and evaporated anyway: by the third morning, Clara sadly acknowledged that her experiment had failed because the houses were decorated with flags, and military bands frightened pigeons away from the plaza with their music. It was May 25, and schoolchildren, a bit embarrassed in their white, crisply starched uniforms without a trace of ink stains, displayed their emblems on their left sides like war decorations. The fatherland over your hearts, as my teacher used to say, and to think how I used to love those big, braided ones with the little shield in the center, and mother made me wear that horrible one she had made herself, with the little crinkled Argentine sash, year after year the same old emblem, why waste money on worthless purchases.. Which, after all is said and done, are the only worthwhile purchases you can make, when you think about it, because useless things aren't expenses – they're a necessity.

She decided that the moment had arrived to buy herself the emblem of her dreams, and right on the corner was one of those men who sold little Argentine flags and other patriotic paraphernalia; but she suddenly came to her senses and changed her mind, thinking it would be better to straighten out her own finances first, since she still had time until July 9 to buy herself a thousand emblems and make herself a necklace. Blue and white, with the eagle in the middle, one wing as blue as the pale, blue sky and the other deep and dark, as blue and storm-tossed as the sea.

She opened her purse, undid the safety pin, and took out the little piece of paper that she had hidden in the lining as a safeguard against enemy eyes. There she had written the address of a very distinguished lady who would find her a job in the provinces, as well as detailed directions for finding that lady.

Lugging her suitcase, she took a streetcar in order to find her place in the world, as the person who had given her the piece of paper had recommended.

There's nothing more pleasant than a streetcar ride. When it's warm outside, cool breezes come in through the windows, and you feel like you're in the middle of the street. When it's cold out, it's like a glass cage, creaking and snoring and purring, carrying you snugly across the city, shielded from the pealing of the bells and the all the commotion. The only bad thing about it is there are lots of old people and pregnant women and all those kinds of people you have to give up your seat for, because if you don't it's shameful. The trick is to grab a window seat so you can look outside and pretend to be distracted. And that's another thing that's so wonderful about riding streetcars: they pass by close to the houses, down narrow streets, skipping over the cobblestones, and you can look at life from the inside out, looking at the geraniums that hang from the windows and sometimes even children peeking through the half-open shutters. Now, *that's* what I call living.

She felt happy. She remembered certain old songs. The stranger had told her she could find work in a distant city, in a very fine house, opposite a park. Just right for her, he had told her. She thought maybe she'd find work as a nanny, because she liked kids. She could take them to the park across the way; she had been dreaming of parks ever since Carlos, since that night she was with him.

When she arrived there, the woman had already moved away. Some of the neighbors thought maybe the police were after her... In her desperation, Clara could hardly appreciate the fate she had been spared.

IV

*A*ssuming that the order of memories should be chronological and not emotional, Clara had arrived at the point where her thoughts shifted back to that subway station and her meeting with Victor. Her happiness at having freed herself from Toño hadn't lasted long. What the hell is freedom good for when you're alone and have no money? She barely had a few coins at the bottom of her purse, hidden in the lining, forgotten coins that no one wanted.

She was in the middle of a vast, blank space, and she couldn't look backward because a strong need to vomit welled up in her mouth, and she couldn't look forward because there was nothing to see there, not even the tiniest of hopes. At the rate she was going, the only thing left for her to do was beg for money. She descended into the subway station.

But her intense hatred and shame distracted her, and she stood there, just thinking, neglecting to hold out her hand. It was at that painful moment that Victor chose to make his appearance in Clara's life.

"Oh, Clara, Clara, excuse me for being a little late. Some nobody held me up with his blathering and wouldn't let me go. What can I tell you – he kept insisting that modern life is all violence and movement, and the only thing that matters is getting ahead! A leftist, a crypto-Communist, whatever... But I didn't say anything; I didn't let him get to me – what for! And he just went on and on, and I couldn't even open my mouth, because if he had let me, I would've fixed him good. He was the hardest hard head I've ever met in my life. A rock – even worse, he was like pure granite. I decided to cut him off, and I took out my catalogues to show him. Forget all that philosophy! Right then and there I put on my salesman's hat, and I didn't listen to one more word of his jabbering. And I, whom he hadn't even allowed to say a single word, gave him my whole spiel about the electric refrigerator. You know, the really impressive one."

"And when I finished, zap! the guy can't find anything better to say than I'm contradicting my own theories, that instead of selling bibles, which is what I ought to be doing, I'm selling electric refrigerators which are just pure noise, with a motor, besides, which means movement, which is a symbol of the future, and there's nothing better than having a good glass of chilled wine or a nice, cold beer when you come home all worn out from running around the streets and going with the flow of modern people, who devote themselves to action, because man controls everything, even electricity, and also that thing where you just push a button and the light goes on and boom! dinner's ready and there's nothing left to do."

"I was all fed up with him. Fed up. There he was, spitting out empty words, meaningless, and I was about ready to go and leave him standing there yammering in front of his own door with all his neighbors watching when suddenly the little light bulb went on in his head, after all, we were just talking about electricity and all that, and he decided to buy the refrigerator after all. He roped himself into it! Nothing like letting the clients talk; no salesman knows that better than I do. They'll do the selling themselves, as long as you let them talk... Of course, he's buying it in small installments. Two years. Imagine! So much hot air, and he doesn't even have enough to pay cash for a crummy refrigerator!"

Clara was about to say something, but Victor paused just long enough to catch his breath: "Speaking of ice boxes, you devil, you haven't even given me a little kiss."

Speaking of ice boxes, you louse, you can go straight to hell, because I'm not about to wait an hour for you just to put up with your stories. But Victor, resourceful as always, took her by the arm and led her to the box office.

"Let's buy ourselves a little fun," he said.

And Clara turned around to see once more the people running toward the station, the English Tower, and the sky which no longer looked like the sea because it was stained with stars.

It was Monday, a bad mood day, beginning of a week whose end was too far off. Inside their respective booths, the amusement park ticket vendors seemed to be asleep, without the slightest hope of getting customers. The giant ferris wheels were empty as they circled around grudgingly, cutting through the thick air, and even the colored lights had lost all their luster. And Victor called that a little fun – baloney!

At the bars inside the "amusement" park, there was only the occasional couple sitting at the open air tables, really dull, and a handful of soldiers looking up as if they wanted to get dizzy by staring at the chained airplanes spinning above their heads. But inside the airplanes there was no one, just a silence produced by a distant, sad tune. A place designed for men, but deserted by them.

Clara made up her mind not to let the depressing atmosphere affect her, and she tried to recapture the happiness she had felt the first time she went up in one of those airplanes that feel almost like they're flying.

She pulled Victor's sleeve: "Come on, let's go on those airplanes – they're so exciting! Let's go on those big ones that fly very high; the ones where you have to climb on a platform to reach them, and if they ever got loose we'd really be flying and then what would it matter if we crashed..."

"You're not telling me you enjoy that nonsense! Explain it to me — what do you feel when you're up there spinning around like a mule at a water wheel?"

"Well, these things are hard to explain. They make me feel like laughing and shouting, and besides I feel a nice kind of dizziness that tickles me inside."

"Bah, if you want to feel that way, let's go screw – it's much nicer."

"It's not the same thing."

"Give me a woman who's content with what she's got, and I'll pass out right here on the spot. Always wanting change, always wanting something new. I ask myself why they were put on this earth..."

"And what do you answer yourself?"

"What?"

"I said, what do you answer when you ask yourself that?"

"You're so exasperating, always trying to get the last word! But if you must know, my answer is that they were put here to make our lives impossible, like those flies that always buzz around you and bother you and even bite you sometimes."

"The ones that bite are horseflies, the males."

"The one who bites me is you. Trying to make me lose control, huh? Getting on my nerves. Who do you suppose makes you say those idiotic things every time you open your mouth? Okay, okay, don't pull that face. C'mon, let's try our luck over there."

And they went over to a kind of skate that you had to propel up a steep metal rail, making it slide down the other side and go up again. Victor paid, blew on his hands, dried them against his pants, grabbed the skate, gave it momentum, and hurled it with ill-concealed effort.

The skate, which was supposed to go around two or three times, didn't even reach the top of the incline. Victor paid again, told Clara that it was a question of skill, not strength, and got ready to try once more. He smiled at the attendants – the ticket vendor and three formidable-looking boys – and was about to launch the skate when his glance fell upon a man in a dark suit and black hat who was hidden in the shadows, leaning against the wall, apparently watching him. His smile stretched out a bit wider, and removing his jacket in order to look better, he launched the skate with all his might.

"Almost twice around!" he exclaimed, satisfied, but the satisfaction vanished from his face when he saw that the stranger wasn't admiring him, but rather Clara, and that she was sneaking glances at him.

He took her by the arm, and said in quite a loud voice: "Let's get out of here, honey; this section is too depressing. Let's go to the dart booth. My aim is first-rate."

As he saw the man following them out of the corner of his eye, he went on, without lowering his voice: "But you already know that. Remember when I came back from the *estancia*? Forty ducks! And that wasn't even counting the partridges. But I prefer duck: with orange sauce, it's the best thing in the world. After turkey, of course."

From her experience with Toño, Clara had learned how to deal with braggarts, so she didn't say a word. Go on, go right ahead, put on your little show. The guy's after *me*..."

"Hey, baby, get rid of that blowhard," the stranger whispered to her after a while, but he turned to leave without waiting for Clara to react. Victor became indignant, picked up his pace, leaving the dart booths behind without looking at them. With a sigh of relief, he bought two tickets for the Haunted Train.

The car pulled away amid whistles and groans, and when it entered the tunnel, Victor embraced Clara, holding her very close. She was preparing for the corpse that popped up out of its coffin at the first curve, but at that moment, Victor kissed her, and she could only feel the threads of the phony spider webs brushing her face. She tried to push him away so she could see the dancing skeletons up close, but Victor, who was getting horny, slipped one hand under her skirt while he rubbed her breasts with the other.

Accompanied by spine-tingling howls and screams, the car plunged ahead, but suddenly, without warning, it emerged from the darkness, coming to a halt at its well-illuminated point of departure.

Clara felt all the heat of the place concentrated in patches on her cheeks, and Victor began to rummage in his pockets, unable to find the tickets. The ticket-taker, who had seen them, was about to make an obscene remark but contained himself in time, remembering that other guy who had smashed up his face. He decided to remain silent, but not before assuming a perfectly, ironic, disgusted smirk.

"Did you see the way that guy was looking at us?" Clara asked.

"Hey, he's just jealous. It really irks those characters to see people having fun while they're working."

Some fun. You'd have to have been really insensitive not to see the sadness of the place, created to produce a happiness that didn't exist.

A woman with dyed hair, dressed in green, sidled up to Victor provocatively, rubbing her thigh against him. He became offended and took Clara by the arm, saying women like that are better off in jail, not walking around loose on the streets.

Most likely he said that to defend Clara, and also to defend himself, but it hurt, anyway. Even since he'd been living with Clara, he professed to hate all streetwalkers mercilessly.

"Let's go somewhere far away from these scumbags and get something to drink."

"We could go dancing!"

"You're getting worse all the time, sweetie. Can't you think of anything better to do than go dancing? Don't you realize that with all this running around on those big machines, the best thing to do is give your body a break and let it rest?"

Well, doesn't he have all the right explanations – no wonder he's such a good refrigerator salesman! It makes me furious, anyway.

"But can't you see there's not even a drop of fun here? Can't you tell it's completely dead, dead and buried? A wake would be much more fun than this; at least there's always some live wire to tell jokes. So if you won't take me dancing, I'm going home, and you can have fun all alone."

The word *alone* was like a magnet that attracted three women who were working the fairgrounds, looking for action. In spite of her anger, Clara realized that her man might not be so bad, after all, but then she remembered how unselective that type of woman was, and she didn't even have a single excuse left to smile about. Victor wasn't smiling, either; he closed his eyes and found himself assaulted by a crowd of prostitutes who tried to snatch his wallet. He walked away rapidly, his eyes closed, and Clara followed, clutching his arm, happy to leave that world of depressing machinery, of mechanical monsters, behind. In the middle of Parque Retiro they found a square, yellow building with a doorman in front. "Come on in, sir, ma'am, the Dance Palace awaits you. Fabulous Argentine and tropical orchestras; luscious cocktails; plenty of fun."

Out of the corner of his eye, Victor spied those two odious women who had followed him there and thought that man must be his guardian angel, opening up the doors to Paradise to him. He took Clara's arm and pushed her inside. The Dance Palace, that sober, limited vision of eternity, offered him salvation.

They sat down at a table near the orchestra. He took out his handkerchief and wiped his forehead.

"What nerve! They follow you even when you're with someone! Those women don't have the slightest bit of respect for anything. They're as sticky as fly-paper, and worst of all, this fly-paper follows its victims instead of waiting quietly somewhere for their victims to fall into the trap by themselves."

Fly-paper, that's great. My mother, who knew about good breeding was, because she washed and ironed for the Brunettis, never hung up those filthy strips. But when she went on vacation to our aunt's house in Quemú-Quemú with the two younger kids, those endless vacations, father let the neighbor ladies convince him – especially the butcher's wife, now I remember – and he hung up some really long strips from one wall of the kitchen to the other. He never took them down again. The butcher's wife must have had some professional bias against flies. Lucky I left all that behind – the ranch house, and the smell of fresh blood that filled it up little by little because the butcher's wife didn't even wash her hands when she came over to visit father.

She had at least a few fragrant, pleasant memories left of Tres Lomas, like when the grocer's delivery boy – the one with curly blond hair, not that thug who took his place – gave her a bouquet of white roses in full bloom, a little wilted, maybe, like the ones the pharmacist's mother (who was a real lady from Santa Rosa de Toay and only came to Tres Lomas the first Friday of the month to visit her son and make confession to the parish priest who was a family friend) wore in her hat. Make friends with the judge, as the saying goes. I never thought it might be worthwhile to make friends with the priest, also. Good idea — think I'll go look for one, become his good friend, and then confess so I won't have to spend the rest of my days praying Hail Mary's and Our Father's to wash away my sins.

Clever thought. She smiled at Victor to show him that occasionally she too was satisfied with herself, and Victor, who liked that smile, asked her to dance, contradicting his own wise counsel for once.

It was the tropical combo's turn to play a mambo. Victor took Clara in his arms and led her around the dance floor with tiny, jerking steps. Passing in front of the musicians, he took two or three turns by himself, and once he even let go of Clara, allowing her to spin alone underneath his arm while he swayed his hips, just as he had seen couples doing in the middle of the dance floor. Clara laughed for no special reason, thoroughly enjoying the way she looked to those men in wide-sleeved white shirts with red ruffles. They were all divine, and they sang and shouted incomprehensible words to the beat of the music. The mambo ended, and they began a samba, but Victor, who couldn't have cared less, continued with the same rhythm, spinning all around the floor at full speed and ending up in front of the stage.

The musicians stopped suddenly to take a break and wipe the saliva from their instruments. Clara and Victor returned to their table holding hands and sat down happily, sighing simultaneously. Victor smiled, and she looked at him affectionately. The waiter seized the moment to approach with his tray under his arm, asking them what they'd like to drink.

"A pint for me. And you?"

"Me too."

"No, Clarita. Get a Primavera – you like those."

Clara couldn't say no. She settled back into her chair. All around her, there were couples laughing and going from one table to another. At the back of the enormous ballroom sat a few solitary men, smoking and drinking with studied dignity: opposite the orchestra, in profile, their chairs backed away from the table and their legs crossed, revealing the well-creased line of their pants legs and their black patent-leather shoes with white suede inserts.

A bit beyond them, she discovered the girls, sitting alone or in pairs, their legs crossed also, with very high-heeled sandals. On their table were long, thin glasses, containing a liquid whose color was as beautiful as sunshine; I'd like to drink it all at once, to get to the kumquat at the bottom. But they're smarter than that: they drink it in little sips; they make it last all night. I'd like order one of those, find out what it's called… Not at all like that dry San Martín that sounds so patriotic but tastes so bitter!

The orchestra members disappeared one by one. A man took the microphone and announced the next group:

"Ladies and gentlemen, next, we're honored to present Julio Ortega (piano arpeggios) and his great Argentine orchestra, featuring a new tango artist, Rubén Chiesa, the San Telmo Kid! And as always, that ever-popular international figure, Carlos del Arrabal! And now, a big round of applause for these giants of the tango!"

Victor didn't applaud, and he looked at him hatefully.

"Tangos! Just when we were getting into the rhythm and we were dancing so well! As if we didn't get enough tangos with half of everything they play on the radio."

Clara was a little disappointed, too. But when the San Telmo Kid came on, singing so earnestly, she felt mollified and paid attention. He wasn't at all good-looking – in fact he was kind of short – but he seemed nice, and surprisingly, his tangos were upbeat. The couples on the dance floor were executing cuts, breaks, and dips, doing fancy footwork while keeping their faces oh-so-calm, with the serious, concentrated expression of people who aren't doing anything at all. Some of the men in the back had approached the single women and now held them very close. They seemed to be dragging themselves onto the floor. Clara wanted to be part of that enormous caterpillar made of human bodies. She asked Victor to dance.

"No, woman, these songs are better for listening than for dancing to."

And she had to resign herself with watching a girl perched on her partner's knee in a *sentadita*, wearing a skirt so tight it looked like it was about to split open.

The San Telmo Kid ended his round with three classic renditions, and Victor took the opportunity to call over the waiter and pay.

"Let's go."

"No, let's stay a little while longer. It's lots of fun. And maybe the next singer will be good."

He looked her over from head to toe as if to embarrass her, adopting a scornful tone: "It's obvious you haven't been working all day like me. Because I can assure you that going from door to door isn't at all relaxing. And you have to wait and argue, and I'm dead tired from so much running around. Right now I'm planning to run on home. We've had enough fun."

He walked away in order to give his words greater weight, and so Clara wouldn't insist. Slowly, she put on her knitted jacket and picked up her purse. Just as she was about to slide her chair back towards the table, the band leader announced Carlos del Arrabal's name, and she felt an urgent need to turn around.

A single instant was enough to bring the sound of Carlos's confident footsteps back to her memory. Carlitos, the same one she had met running between the tables at Don Mario's café. And she realized that if lately she had hardly even given him a thought, it was because she carried him deep within herself, together with the certainty of meeting him again someday. And then one night there he was, just like that, without a warning, without any previous signs, taking her completely by surprise. She had to lean against the back of the chair and breathe deeply in order to regain her hold on reality. But his image didn't dissolve; he was still there on the platform, adjusting the microphone cord and getting ready to sing. The band members were tuning their instruments, but above the noise Clara heard her own heart pounding in her chest.

Merely by closing her eyes, she could see Palermo Park, the moon, and Carlos standing before her. It was inevitable that she would meet him again because the last time they had never reached the lake, and the swans were still waiting for them. She opened her eyes again and managed to smile at him. He smiled, too, showing his white teeth, but Clara didn't accept that smile, which was directed at everyone in general. She wondered why his heart wasn't pounding as well, betraying her presence, but maybe it was just as well, because Victor was with her now, summoning her from the doorway with desperate gestures.

She headed for the exit, but she couldn't resist the temptation to turn around once more and look at the enormous, naked ballroom in which only Carlos's body was illuminated under the beams of the opaque spotlights. Then she quickened her steps in order to leave before Carlos's voice might attract her to him once more.

The uniformed doorman handed her a small pink card, which she placed in her jacket pocket automatically, without checking to see what it was all about.

Once outside, Victor took her arm: "What took you so long?"

"I had a little more Primavera left in my glass, and I wanted to finish it so it wouldn't go to waste."

Transition

I

*T*he card simply said:

The management of the Dance Palace thanks you for your patronage and hopes to see you again in our ballroom during the week. By presenting this card to your waiter, you will receive a delicious complimentary cocktail, especially prepared for you by our bartender and it was printed. Nevertheless, Clara still retained the warmth that had been running up and down her spine all night long, as well as the anxiety of deciphering the contents of that card, which she had so carelessly left in her jacket pocket. She'd spent the whole night in uncertainty, while Victor slept at her side, sometimes snoring and sometimes moaning in his sleep. She didn't want to get up and risk waking him and be forced to reveal her secret to him. The card might well contain a message from Carlos, who had seen her before he went on stage; one could make such lovely assumptions about what it might say, imagining phrases like: *Clara, I love you – return to my arms;* or simply *I'll wait for you tomorrow at 6:30; or Don't come back. You make me suffer.*

She imagined Carlos looking for her in all the waterfront bars, finding her at last in the Dance Palace, together the two of them singing an endless love duet like in that Technicolor movie she had seen a few days earlier. She would put on her lavender dress, the same one she wore that night in the park, which looked like the one the woman in the movie wore, and little by little they would form their own band, inscribing their entwined initials,

C&C, on the drum in the percussion section.

She painstakingly tried to forget about Carlos's wife, the one who had ruined all her plans two years before, and for the first time in her life tried to imagine happiness in all its multiple possibilities and from various angles. First she was with Carlos on a beach, right by the sea; then in a little house in the woods, very charming and neatly furnished; finally with him in the bar at the lake, sitting very close together. She always wore her lavender dress and he always sang sweet love songs in her ear.

He serenaded her so soothingly that Clara fell asleep. When she awoke, she was astonished to realize that it was already 10:30 in the morning and Victor had gone out. She became frightened, thinking he might have stolen her pink card, and she leaped up to look for it. Luckily, she found it exactly where she had put it, and her relief helped her overcome her disappointment at not finding even a single word from Carlos on it. Ultimately, she decided that Carlos was like the rest of them after all, those who don't believe too much in true love. Victor didn't believe in those things, either, but he was generous with her: he gave her a roof over her head and food, and he didn't ask her for anything, or hardly anything, in exchange. And he had to love her a little – if not, there would be no reason for him to put up with her. She decided it wouldn't be fair to be unfaithful to him, even if it was only in her imagination. She went to the bathroom to get his dirty shirts and began to wash them.

"How dirty a traveling salesman gets," she sighed in a very quiet voice, in order not to disturb His Highness Sir Silence, her friend.

She left the shirts hanging over the bathtub to drip and remembered that other shirt which needed its collar turned. She went over to the wardrobe, and upon opening the dirty clothes drawer, she discovered her lavender dress, which Victor had forbidden her to wear because the neckline was too low. She was tempted to try it on to see if it still fit her, but then she told herself she'd be better off worrying about her housework and not dreaming so much.

Victor returned at twelve-thirty and found her sewing. Lunch wasn't ready.

"What's the matter, can't you see I'm hungry?" he shouted, without greeting her. It's obvious you don't do anything here all day long. And the table's not even set! It's always when a person's in a hurry that nothing is ever ready!"

Clara took the plates and silverware out of the cupboard without a word. She put them on the kitchen table and removed the cold meat from the refrigerator.

"Cold cuts, cold cuts!" he shouted. For days we've been eating the same cold cuts. I wonder how you'd manage if my company hadn't loaned me one of their refrigerators. Lucky for you – this way you can keep food in it for months!"

Clara shrugged her shoulders. She was surprised to note how little Victor's angry outbursts affected her. Before, when she still held out hope for him, she had been bewildered by him, had wanted to hit him, or bite him, or tear him apart. Now, however, she felt nothing, and she was puzzled by her lack of reaction. She was no longer herself; she was someone else who had invaded her skin.

"Look, I'll make you some nice mayonnaise, just the way you like it. And I'll fix you a salad with garlic."

"Garlic! Are you crazy, woman? With all the customers I have to visit today? And in Rivadavia, a classy neighborhood, on the Olivos train line."

There was a pause as he sliced himself a generous hunk of salami. He removed the skin, placed the salami on a slice of buttered bread, and added, with his mouth full: "But you can go ahead and make me that mayonnaise…"

As she beat the egg yolks, she thought of asking Victor if his company sold blenders, too, but she saw him eating with such relish that she chose to remain silent. He dispatched the cold cuts, the salad, and two bananas. Only when he was drinking his coffee, standing in the doorway, did he realize that Clara hadn't eaten anything.

"Hey, you didn't even take a mouthful. What's eating you now? Are you angry?"

"No, not me. Why should I be angry?"

"Nothing, I just meant… Listen, tonight I'll be home late; I have a meeting with my co-workers because early tomorrow I'm going to Mercedes. Eat something and go to the movies – that'll change your ideas a little. In the drawer of the nightstand there's a fifty-peso bill. Take it and go have some fun for a while. Lately you've been looking like your best friend died."

And he left without even kissing her goodbye.

What's the point of working, just to be turned into a slave? Clara said to herself while she ate the leftover salami, sucking on the string. With a piece of bread, she wiped up the mayonnaise remaining on the plate and ate the last banana. Then she went to the bathroom to look at herself in the mirror above the sink and take inventory: young, no rolls of fat or wrinkles or anything; perfectly nice-looking – maybe a bit anemic, if you looked inside her lower eyelid, but who goes around turning people's eyelids inside out in order to assess their health?

Sometimes, it's true, they stare at you, as if they wanted to penetrate your soul, but that's all, nothing like going too far, nothing like delving into other people's intimacy, because that's dangerous and wrong – you could run the risk of falling in love. As though you could fall in love with defects! No, that's not it – you don't fall in love with defects, but rather with the fact that you know all the other person's defects and their weaknesses, and you share them. But let's get back to the business at hand: supple body, narrow waist, pretty legs. With the lavender dress and the new bra I could look divine.

She hurried to the bedroom, where the narrow wardrobe mirror revealed her full-length reflection, concealing her broad hips. She looked at herself in front view and from the back: full buttocks and ample breasts – not bad at all. She could be an artist's model. Or the inspiration for a tango singer…

She reached out her hand to the drawer where the dress was, but the voice of reason made her stop in mid-gesture, sending her back into the kitchen where she had left the shirt with the ripped collar lying on a chair. She took a razor blade and began to attack the cuffs, which were worn out as well.

"Everything's worn out; everything's worn out," she hummed. Even Victor, who shows up, yells, and takes off. Wo-o-o-orn out."

But she stopped short, before she could feel too sorry for herself. Why complain so much? It wasn't that bad here. It had been worse before. Now everything is stable, respectable, and insubstantial. Respectable. And yet I complain. I'm a hard-hearted, ungrateful, miserable wretch. Poor Victor must work like a dog with his damn customers, and things don't always work out for him. Damn razor blade won't even cut! But, after all, he has no reason to inflict his bad moods on me, as if I were running around all day long and didn't have the house as neat as a pin for him! Like that time he got home at god-knows-what time and found me up. How you doin'? D'you go to the movies? he says to me, as cool as can be. And I say, No, man, I was washing down the kitchen walls; they were all greasy. Don't you see how they shine? Not bad, not bad, but you could have finished the job. You left a streak on this wall up here… Men don't realize that a girl can't always reach perfection, or even the ceiling, sometimes!

She interrupted herself and raised her eyes: the razor blade that didn't cut the thread had managed to insert itself forcefully into her left thumb. Without daring to look at the cut, she stuck her finger in her mouth and began to suck on it carefully. The taste of blood, nauseating and warm, made her want to vomit. The shirt was stained with bright red drops that soon would turn brown and crusty. She remembered the stains that were left on the sheet after her first time, with that sailor; she remembered how hard it had been to wash them out the next morning, to hide the evidence, and she ran to the bathroom to stick the shirt under the faucet. She still had the razor blade in her hand; she felt like crushing it. She broke it into little pieces, instead, and flushed them down the toilet. So delicate, as treacherous as a skinny woman. Luckily my father shaved with a straight razor – much safer. He used to get so angry when I used it to sharpen my pencils. Victor, what do you expect, shaves with an electric razor. It's faster, true, but it's much less romantic. No soap, no foam, no funny faces. And it doesn't even shave off the whiskers all the way down – the ones that are left are hard and they hurt.

In order to stanch the blood that was still running down the side of her hand, she put her finger under the faucet. The stream of cold water felt good; she didn't feel the heat and throbbing any more. She tied a handkerchief tightly around it, and it stopped bleeding.

She went over to the window. The warm air made her feel like going outside to look November in the face. Only a single gesture, perhaps just one step, separated her from the night stand where the fifty-peso bill was waiting. She sat down on the bed. The gas and electric bills were all in an orderly pile, clipped together, but refrigerator brochures, all spread out, spilled from the drawer. Clara looked for the money, finding it in a paperback edition of *How to Win Friends and Influence People*, the only book in the house.

The bill was new, green, and as crisp as dry leaves. Clara picked it up with both hands and thought that the piece of paper transmitted unknown pleasure. She held it up to the light, discovering the image of a general hidden inside the oval. She felt bad about spending a brand-new bill like that: they'd give her some dirty, pawed-over bills in exchange.

Victor had told her to go to the movies to change her thoughts a little, but she didn't want to change her thoughts, no matter how bad they were, for others that didn't belong to her. She wanted to hold on to everything: the new bill and her old thoughts. Besides, she had no reason to create more expenses for poor Victor.

Suddenly she realized that all her scattered thoughts revolved around that pink card. By simply reaching out her arm, she could find it in her jacket pocket. It wasn't new, like the bill, and its edges were worn out and gray. She wouldn't mind giving it up at all, and the free cocktail could be a big savings. She had some loose change in her wallet to pay her carfare. She imagined she might have to dance with strange men, but after all she'd done with strange men, dancing was the least of her worries.

She would see Carlos again... She stopped for a moment in the middle of the room, trying to imagine the feeling she'd get seeing him again. She was afraid she wouldn't be able to speak when the moment arrived, that a knot would form in her throat, choking her. The best thing to do, she thought, would be to stay home and sew. But then she scolded herself for being such a coward, telling herself that if she didn't go it was because she really was afraid Carlos would reject her, or force her to leave the comfort of her current situation.

At four-thirty she finally decided to go to Parque Retiro to see him again. She wouldn't speak to him or anything; she's sit at a table in the back, just to hear him sing. By seven PM she still wasn't ready. She climbed up on a table to reach the box on top of the wardrobe, where she looked for her new bra. It was the only one that looked good with the lavender dress because it revealed the top of her breasts, an area that so offended Victor's sense of modesty.

Then she had to iron the dress, which had a flounce, and iron her special slip. When she was finished, she decided to lie down for a while so her face wouldn't look tired, but she could only tolerate being in bed for five minutes. It took her almost an hour to put on her makeup and pluck her eyebrows, and she got on the bus with the firm resolution of not to approach Carlos. No matter what.

II

Some of her old, forgotten sense of shame returned to her when she handed the pink card to the waiter. Modesty and circumspection – what out-of-place virtues those were in the Dance Palace. However, there were few people there to notice her embarrassment. She sat down at the table farthest from the band and attentively listened to the Brazilian rhythms played by the musicians dressed as Cubans. After just a little while, a guy with a handkerchief tied around his neck asked her to dance. She reluctantly stood up (she didn't like to offend anyone) and stepped out onto the dance floor. To shake her bones. Take a few turns around. Polish the floor. But her mind was elsewhere: she stepped on the handkerchief guy's foot two or three times before the song ended, and he walked her back to her table with a sigh of relief.

I was in too much of a hurry; I never know how to do things right. I got here too early, and what I *don't* want to do is wait, always wait. And maybe today is Carlos's day off. He's not going to come. I ought to go back home; I've got too much to do to be wasting my time here. This is crazy. Or maybe he'll come, but with his wife.

When she thought of Carlos's wife, she felt afraid. Her heart started to pound. It was all on account of that neckline, which was too low. There was no reason to go around exhibiting herself like that. The waiter had already served her the cocktail especially prepared by the bartender, but she couldn't touch it. It would be better to run away, quickly, now, during the break, to go before they announced the tango orchestra and probably Carlos's name. She pick up her purse to leave.

From a neighboring table, a girl had been watching her; on seeing her get ready to leave, she decided to approach.

"You new here?"

"Yeah," said Clara, hesitatingly, after a pause.

"That's why you're getting bored. I'm bored today, too. Wouldja like me to sit with you and we can talk a little?"

She went to get her drink, and she sat down without waiting to be asked.

"But don't think I've just been sittin' around keepin' the chair warm. I danced the whole time! I'm wiped out, like they say. That crazy music hurts my feet. If you're not careful, you could even get blisters. Mine already feel like an open sore. Lucky the tangos come next... more relaxing, right?"

There are some questions that are just impossible to answer. The other woman took a few sips of her drink and shook her curly, brown mane with the wide bleached streak on the left side.

"My name's María Magdalena. Monona to my friends and to other women. And you?"

"Clara."

"Nice name, but it don't fit you, does it? Trouble is, you're new in this business, you're just new. Me, on the other hand, I know this scene like the back of my hand. I can tell you anything you wanna know. I don't know why, I swear, but I took a liking to you right away. It must be that innocent face of yours. But you're not innocent, are you?"

"No."

"Just as well. There's no room here for shrinkin' violets. You gotta be shrewd in this life, honey. And for sure in the next one, too. If not, some dumb broad comes along and robs you of the best locations. Just because she's quicker'n you, which don't mean she's got more gray matter or nothin', like they say. I fought hard and steady to be what I am. One of these days I'll tell you all about it..."

She finished off her drink in one gulp and summoned the waiter with a nod of her head. The same thing, she said, pointing to the two long, narrow glasses. Clara had hardly touched hers, but the other woman insisted that she finish it and order another one. Clara obeyed, noticing sadly that they were taking away the kumquat which she had left untouched in the bottom of the glass.

"But the card says just one free drink..."

"It don't matter. This one's on me. I'm dyin' of thirst – you'll see how good another drink'll taste."

The waiter brought them over. Monona drank half of hers right away.

"At least it does me good. Cacho didn't come today, see? No, how could you understand anything! You're new here. Otherwise you'd know by now that Cacho isn't here, so the place is a goddamn bore. He's the life of the party. And he's mine, y'know, even if he does take off every so often with every floozy he can find around here. That don't matter to me – after all, a girl has her little flings, too, 'cause you gotta earn a living somehow, like Cacho. But today it was my turn to have him, and he didn't show up. You think he's jealous of the guy I picked up yesterday? A real macho, the kind with muscles like *empanadas*. But Cacho knows *he's* the one for me, even though I never tell him, 'cause he's so conceited to begin with. Listen to me, with guys you gotta go around acting all mysterious; if not, they won't even look at you."

Clara made every effort to listen to her and answer her, though the San Telmo Kid had already started to sing, and she knew that in a little while it would be Carlos's turn. She sipped her drink slowly to gain time, and when she reached the bottom, she tried to fish out the kumquat, which had stubbornly remained stuck to the bottom of the glass, with her tongue.

Monona shut up for a moment and looked at her distrustfully before deciding to ask: "But if you're not one of us, what the hell are you doin' here anyway?"

"I'm a friend of Carlos del Arrabal," Clara replied triumphantly, with the kumquat still in her mouth.

"Carlos's little friend! You don't say!" She burst out laughing vigorously, shaking her breasts and nearly wailing. She could barely contain herself; she was practically choking, and Clara, not knowing what to do, slapped her on the back while Monona waggled a finger at her, shouting, "You, you!" between hiccups. Clara was quite frightened, imagining what Carlos might have said about her. Horrible things, no doubt, that give you chills and make you laugh at the same time like the Haunted Train. I want to know, quick, calm down, will you? She shook her harder and harder, which only succeeded in intensifying Monona's laughter.

Finally, Monona withdrew a handkerchief from her cleavage and blew her nose, then dried the tears from her eyes.

"So you're Carlos's secret lover... That's one of the funniest things I've ever heard! If you could have heard how he described you: loaded with jewels, with an enormous bun. A la-dy, for your information, everyone, not like the rest of you bimbos. Can you imagine? Funny, fu-u-n-n-ny! You're just like the rest of us, a poor little fish, no better, no worse. Worse, maybe. And he said you went around in a limo with a chauffeur, no less. Some swelled head he's got! Take it from me!"

"Maybe he wasn't talking about me," Clara ventured, although the idea didn't please her at all. "Maybe he was talking about some other woman."

"Oh, no. Don't give me that, honey. Don't try to cover it up now.

He was going around saying in that tango singer voice of his that you were unique, special, that you took up all his time, that you didn't let him breathe, he said. All that just to avoid paying attention to us lowlifes. What a bullshitter! Cacho suspected as much because he really knows how to size people up. He told me more than once, more than once. That little tango singer runs away from skirts 'cause he's impotent. Sexually damaged, like he says so nicely. That's what it must be. If not, he wouldn't go around showing off about a broad like you. But Cacho, for your information, isn't impotent at all, just the opposite. One day you'll find out if you meet him; he's like that with all the women. He says men have an obligation to comfort women, 'cause if they don't, the broads get all hysterical and nobody can put up with them, and in order to comfort them you have to take advantage of them and also be taken advantage of. He'll explain it to you real good. He's full of theories. And he hangs around with me a lot – he was supposed to show up today. You wanna tell me why he didn't come?"

"Umm… maybe something happened to him. An accident?"

Monona lifted her head and shook her mane.

"That's gotta be it, an accident, sure. If not, he'd be here already. A little accident, of course, a few bruises or somethin' like that. He must be fighting with everybody there, so they'll pay to get his suit cleaned, or whatever. He always gets something out of it – he's so sharp… Of course, he won't be in no condition to dance. He'll pick me up at closing time, for sure."

Clara looked at her, horrified. The San Telmo Kid was already in the middle of his third song. Next, Carlos would come on, and she'd didn't know what to do, what kind of expression to assume. Suddenly, Monona remembered her and asked:

"Hey, tell me something. That Carlos doesn't know you're here, right? He must've forbidden you to come, because you'll make him choke on his own bullshit. Now he really put his foot in it; now he won't be able to go around showing off. Did he tell you to come?"

"How could he tell me anything, if the last time I saw him was ages ago, and he didn't even dream he'd be singing anywhere? But yesterday I happened to be here with another gentleman and I saw him again. The thing between us was a long time ago."

"Oh, yeah? Then it's true about the rich old bag?"

"How should I know? When I met him, he was a simple guy; he waited tables in a nice bar. I only knew him a little until one night he took me to the park and then I really got to know him. It was fantastic."

"Were you a virgin?"

"No, a hooker."

There was a pause.

"Hmmm..." Monona replied. "But he was the one for you. Tell me, did you see him again? I'll bet he took all your dough and split." "No, he didn't take a cent from me. He just went away, that's all. His wife locked him up in the house or something." "Oh, so he's married, besides! Great! This will really make Cacho laugh. And you, you're in love with that squawker... Well, there's no accounting for tastes; we all scratch where it itches. And you never saw him again?"

"No."

"Then why do you say you're his friend? If you made friends with every guy who laid on top of you..."

"You can't understand these things. He's different because I love him."

"Whadda you mean, I can't understand? As tight as I am with Cacho? Look, just so you'll see I'm not a bitch, as soon as he finishes yapping, I'll call him over and tell him to come see you. The Dance Palace, ladies and gentlemen, honored by a great love! Ugh!"

The announcer's voice had just pronounced his name. "Carlos," Clara repeated, and then she thought about Monona's last words and she shouted: "No! I don't want to see him!" She thought an explanation was necessary. "I'm with another guy now, and he'll get jealous."

"And what the hell do you care about the other guy if this one is the one you like?"

"That's the least of it, whether I like him or not, because the other guy wants to marry me."

"Marry you?" Monona started to laugh again. "Marry you?... Don't you know there's no such thing as marriage for women like us? When you're born a whore, you die a whore."

"But I wasn't born a whore. Things just turned out that way, that's all. When I was little I went to Mass every Sunday. That's why I don't want to see Carlos."

"Look at her! How wild! it's not surprising, with that name of yours. Clara... a nun's name."

Just then Clara turned pale and held her breath.

"Be quiet, he's coming on stage," she whispered, pressing Monona's arm, but Monona kept on talking, indifferent to Clara's turmoil as she grasped the table to keep from shouting out, to keep from calling him. The band struck up the first notes of *El Choclo*. Clara knew all the words; they could have sung them together. Carlos was wearing a blue suit with a carnation in his lapel, and she felt her whole body stretching towards him.

But Monona was implacable: "Clara... a name like that's confusing; no guy would dare touch a woman named Clara. On the other hand, look at me: Cacho named me María Magdalena. It's an old story – one of the oldest whores in the world. She followed Christ around, but Christ didn't even give her the time of day 'cause he was a serious guy. But now serious guys are as scarce as hen's teeth, and any crackpot with an ounce of common sense realizes that's not my name by accident. You can't go around hiding things in this life, honey; you are what you are, and it's no use trying to make a silk purse out of a sow's ear..."

Carlos had already begun to sing, with a low, resonant voice, just as Clara expected, but the other woman's words pounded in her temples like a rattle. She tried to create a barrier of silence around her, a barrier that would only let in Carlos's voice. But it was impossible.

"Of course, people who know me don't have to use such a long name. Cacho invented the nickname Monona, too. I have lots of names, like artists and crooks. If he ever meets you, Cacho'll give you another name, for sure, you'll see. If I told you my name was Daisy... Nothing more ridiculous. Cacho says daisies are okay for pigs; that's why he told me that story and gave me the name. Because even if he doesn't look like it, he's a very smart man who knows a lot. He'll tell you also that your neckline isn't bad, but that a full skirt like that is only for convent school. Cacho really knows about things; you gotta be tough, honey, if you don't want people to step all over you."

Let them step on me; let them step on me and crush me, but let me listen to him in peace. She stretched her neck, moving her head from side to side; she hunched down like a turtle in its shell to get away from Monona's voice attacking her. Carlos, Carlos, just like Gardel.

"Be quiet, do me a favor, just be quiet," she managed to say at last. She felt like crying with frustration.

"You want to listen to that nincompoop, I understand. But make an effort and try to understand me; if Cacho was here, he'd have you listening till you couldn't take it any more. But Cacho didn't show up, and I've gotta talk with someone or I'll explode. Look, I swear I'll bring him over to you when he's done yelping, but don't make me listen to him now, 'cause he gives me hysterics."

Clara felt like digging her nails in deep and pulling off Monona's skin, but she waited for Carlos to finish his song before saying in a slow, restrained voice:
"I don't want him to come over. I'm telling you, I don't want him to. Jesus!"
The waiter approached cautiously.
"Two more."
"You still owe me for the other two."
"Stop acting dumb and bring me what I asked for."
Clara tried to hear the name of Carlos's next number, but she couldn't catch it. Meanwhile, the waiter stood there, not knowing what to do.
"I'm telling you, bring 'em over, will ya? If I can't pay you, Cacho will."
"Not a chance! Cacho never wants to get involved with other people's bills, least of all women's. I don't blame him, he knows them well…"
Clara managed to catch a few phrases of the waltz Carlos was singing, and it was just like that time when he whispered words in her ear on the way to the park.
Everyone was chattering around her, and she would have liked to stand up indignantly, strike her fist against the table, and shout at everyone to shut up, but she had only enough nerve to curl up even more in her chair.
"Son of a bitch! I hope you drop dead!" Monona spat out at the waiter, at the exact moment when Carlos dragged out the last word of the song, Gardel-style. A fury-filled silence descended.
"That bastard won't bring me any booze 'cause he says I've got no dough. As if I ever burned anyone. He's a cheap creep, but I'm gonna tell Cacho, I swear on my mother, I'm gonna tell, and then he'll really get it. No one messes with Cacho's woman."
And changing her tone: "Clara, sweetie, wouldn't you have a couple of pesos hidden in there somewhere to buy me a drink with?"
"I don't feel like drinking any more."
"You never feel like doin' nothing. You've got ice water in your veins, that's what. You don't want another cocktail; you don't wanna

see that tango singer. I'm telling you, you don't know how to live. I wonder why there's even people like you in this world."

Clara drank her cocktail angrily. Between clenched teeth, she said:

"What I want is for you to shut up, for the love of God. At least let me listen to this last song."

They had already announced a new number, Che, Amarroto, and Carlos had taken the microphone in hand again. Disturbing sparks appeared in Monona's eyes.

"I'll shut up if you buy me another drink. And pay for the ones I owe, too, 'cause I came without money today."

"I have no money, either," she answered, sighing.

"What d'ya mean, you've got no money, you little twit! Get outta here… A sensible girl like you doesn't go around without a cent. You look like a thrifty type, honey, so don't give me that baloney. Pay him, and I swear I'll shut up: not one more word until that donkey stops braying. I swear on my life."

Carlos deserved that much, at least. Slowly she opened her purse and took out the fifty pesos. She hardly looked at them, but when she passed the bill from one hand to the other, it crackled like a dry leaf.

Monona kept her word. She finished her new drink in one gulp and then plunged her head between her crossed arms on top of the table and stifled a few sighs. Clara was able to relax in her chair, half close her eyes, catch her breath. She felt disappointed when Carlos didn't sing a love song like the previous one, but rather a comical tango, judging from the words. She opened her eyes, disoriented, but he was still there, and that brought back her feelings of happiness. Then came the words of the tango, and she rolled up the bills as if she were making a salami. The words sounded prophetic, and she knew she had done the right thing by sacrificing the new bill for Carlos. Mustn't be a tightwad: with money you can buy everything, even a bit of peace.

She looked at Monona with disgust, but immediately returned her gaze to her Carlos, so radiant beneath the spotlights, and suddenly her heart was in her mouth and she thought she would cry for joy.

When Carlos del Arrabal had finished his last tango, Clara didn't even have the strength to applaud. Some youngsters who had been dancing began to shout, Encore! Encore! and Clara supported them heartily in her mind, but she didn't want to part her lips for fear of breaking the spell.

Suddenly the lights dimmed, and the stage was empty. Monona leaped up: "Now I'll bring him over to you so you can get it off your chest."

"No! I don't want to see him…" but the other woman had already walked away, muttering to herself.

Clara remained there, her gaze fixed on a vague point in the distance, her arms resting in her lap, unable even to decide if what was about to happen was vital or unimportant. She didn't realize that Monona had disappeared behind the same little door that had swallowed up the musicians; everything seemed fuzzy on account of those three cocktails she had been forced to drink. You mustn't think; you mustn't think.

"Clara… Good evening."

Carlos's tall silhouette obscured the lights, and when Clara raised her eyes, she couldn't see his expression, which had remained in shadows. He no longer sparkled as he had under the spotlights, and his gestures were bland, indecisive. Clara melted because she sensed how vulnerable he was; behind him, Monona narrowed her eyes ironically. All of that – her irony, his vulnerability, the fact she couldn't see Carlos's face, the three cocktails – gave her courage, and she heard herself say, as if she were in a world where things were plain and simple: "Why, Carlos. How are you?"

And she stretched out her hand in a perfect gesture of perfect courtesy. He grasped it in his soft, sweaty one, and Clara realized that he needed her indifference. So she went on: "I didn't want to bother you, but this lady kept insisting."

"Thank you, Clara, thank you."

Monona didn't want to be left out: "Bah, bah! Enough beating around the bush. Let's have a drink to celebrate the great reunion. Order me a gin while I go to the toilet. Back in a flash."

She got up hesitatingly and walked away, wiggling her hips.

"She's drunk," Clara remarked, half to herself.

"She's always drunk," Carlos replied, also half to himself. Then he reacted, saying as he took Clara's hand, "Clara, my sweet Clarita. What have you been doing with yourself all this time? How did you find me here?"

Clara lost her composure. She could only say, "Carlos!" emptying the entire content of her lungs into the air.

"I thought about you so much, Clara. When I remembered that night, I felt bad. I don't know why, but nothing had ever seemed as important to me as the time we spent together. Did you think so, too? Did you?"

"Ssshh, she's coming back."

"We have to get away from that lowlife, right now. She's unbearable."

"Let's escape from here."

"There's no time. Look, tell her that Cacho is looking for her. She'll believe you. Tell her he sent for her, or something like that."

"But I can't, it's not true."

"Tell her for my sake, invent any old story..." and he let go of the hand he held between his own.

"Whew! Now I feel better," Monona exclaimed, flopping down in a chair. "Where's my gin?"

Beneath the table, Carlos's leg found Clara's and wound itself around hers, beseechingly. Then she raised her eyes with an expression of purest innocence, and said: "A man was here looking for you. He said Cacho was waiting for you."

"Cacho? Where?"

"Umm... he didn't say. I think he said in the usual place, or something like that."

"What did the guy look like?"

"I didn't notice. Dark, a mustache, I think. I didn't think it was all that important."

"Not important! You stupid bitch! Cacho is waiting for me; he sent for me... I have to run."

She picked up her purse and left at full speed, stumbling over tables and chairs. When he saw her disappear through the revolving door, Carlos couldn't contain himself and burst out laughing. Clara looked and him sadly, and then she sighed.

"She was laughing at you, too, just a little while ago."

Surprised, Carlos stopped laughing and looked directly into her eyes.

"That harpy was laughing at me? And what did she tell you? That woman is worse than a viper. More poisonous, too. Give her a stick and she'll curl around it. I can't understand how she can be a friend of yours. But you must know her pretty well, and you must really know Cacho. How long have you been running around with that Cacho guy?"

"What do you mean, I must know them? I've never seen Cacho in my life."

"And that business about the usual place. How do you know about any usual place?"

"Well, lovers always have a place where they usually meet, right? At least that's what I think."

"Why are you asking me? I don't know anything about this kind of stuff. You, on the other hand, seem to be very familiar with the things lovers do."

A reproachful silence descended, during which Clara tried to think of a barbed remark about Carlos's rich lover. Finally, she told herself that the truth would be more painful for her than for him, and so she simply ventured: "Don't be so hard; if you only knew what she told me about you…"

"Don't mention that viper to me! Everyone here hates me because I don't pay any attention to them. The only thing I ask is that they leave me alone, that all the hookers in Parque Retiro leave me alone."

Clara bit her lower lip.

"Forgive me, Clara, I didn't mean you. You're completely different. Different from any other woman I've ever met. You're nicer and more innocent than all of the ones who think they're so pure. You can't imagine how much I've thought about you since my wife died."

There was another long silence after which Clara could manage only to murmur, "Poor Carlos!" because a mixture of pity and joy prevented her from seeing clearly in this matter of the death of the woman who had kept them apart.

"Come on, Clarita, let's get out of here. What do you say we go for a walk down by the port? I'll tell you everything. Do you have time?"

"Of course," she replied, without thinking of the time or of Victor.

All the rides had been shut down at the amusement park, forming a thousand shadowy corners made for kissing, but Carlos kept on walking, guiding her by the shoulders, and he didn't stop until he had pushed her through the turnstile. Suddenly, Clara found herself facing the familiar scenery of the English Tower, the large, grassy quad, and the train station in the distance.

They walked along in silence towards the port, her heels catching in the cobblestones. They were still far from the docks, although a few illuminated masts were visible. Clara thought that it would be best for them to walk quite a distance, in order to get away from everything they had experienced until now, in order to begin a new life washed clean of the sticky baggage of the past. But Carlos insisted on revealing another aspect of the past, which clung to her body like a tick.

"Do you remember Don Mario's hotel? We were doing fine there, huh? We could have seen each other often and run away to the park once in a while, like that time. But when I returned home that same night, my wife already knew everything. The other stupid waiter told her that he had seen me going out with you. A whore, he told her. Please excuse me; he was a jerk. And she, who had always controlled me, she made me give it all up, she forced me to. She had a very weak heart, and any little thing made her sick. And she was my wife, after all, and I couldn't just kill her, right? When we got married, she looked so lovely dressed all in white. But all I have left of that day is a memory, because she never put on that dress again, or any other one. She spent the whole day in her bathrobe with her hair uncombed, maybe because of her illness. After all, she was my wife, and I couldn't kill her..."

They passed by a wooden barracks and heard sailors' voices inside, singing in a foreign language. It's true, then, that there are exotic lands when millions of people I'll never meet live. Would it be so awful after all to kill one of all those people who live in the world, like ants?

Carlos went on with his confession: "You know, before I got married, I was a tango singer, like now. But my wife didn't want me to keep singing, and she found me that waiter's job. The money wasn't bad, counting tips, but when she found out I had gone out with you, she went crazy animal made a real stink of it. You can't imagine how she shouted, till she turned purple and started choking. Luckily the druggist came over right away and gave her a shot, but later I had to swear to her that I'd never see you again. She must have smelled danger; she knew I liked you... Then she found me a job as an usher in a movie house on Corrientes Street. Always jobs with tips! But it was fun, until she got jealous again, and whenever I didn't show up at home at exactly the right time, she called the movie house to see if it was true I was delayed, or if I had gone out with some girl. The guys teased me so much that one night I did go out with a girl just so they'd see I wasn't afraid. When I got home, she was lying in bed, hardly even breathing. By the time I called the druggist, it was already too late: she died early the next morning."

Clara felt sorry for Carlos. She took his hand and brought it to her lips to kiss.

"I'm so sorry," she said. "If you'd like, one day we'll go to the cemetery and bring her flowers."

"But you must hate her. She was the one who kept us apart. Or doesn't that matter to you?"

Clara would have liked to reply that it did, that it mattered to her more than anything else, but she was embarrassed and instead explained as though she were talking to a child: "You should never hate the dead. They're over on the other side. We have to love them now and be good to them because they can't do anything to us, anyway."

"Yes,…but let me tell you the rest. I felt terribly guilty when she died, but a doctor who had seen her not long before told me that it was inevitable, that she couldn't have lasted much longer anyway with that disastrous heart of hers. Who would have guessed it – she could yell louder than anyone, and she seemed so imposing! When the doctor told me that, my guilty feelings went away, and I began to feel happy. Yes, you heard me right, happy. Because at last I was free, after all those long years. After a month of mourning, I went to see my old friend the band leader, and they hired me right away. You've got to earn a living somehow… But I began to feel lonely. You don't know what it's like to go home to a boarding house and not to find anyone there to talk to you, or even to yell at you. All the noise you hear belongs to other people; the walls are so thin… When I hear the neighbors fighting, I miss my wife. But instead of thinking about my wife, I almost always think about you, in what you might be doing at that moment, in how happy we would have been together."

He stopped to light a cigarette, and Clara sat down on one of the hitching posts because she was tired. He squatted at her side, burying his face in her lap.

"I looked for you everywhere, Clarita. I even decided to go to Don Mario's hotel, and the poor guy told me you had moved away a long time ago, and that it was my fault. I felt so sad. He was sad, too, and I had to promise him that if I ever found you again, I'd take you to see him. Do you want to go tomorrow?"

Clara felt sorry for Don Mario, too, but she didn't want to be returned to her past now that she had decided to begin a new life.

"No, Carlos, not tomorrow. Some other time. Let me get used to seeing you before I see Don Mario."

She stood up. "Let's go back now, I'm tired."

"But you're not offended, are you? You know I love you."

She wondered why he didn't kiss her, if he loved her. Love must be something strange that I haven't discovered yet. What can I do to understand feelings inside out and upside down? She tried not to think about the rich woman Monona had mentioned, and she told herself that Carlos belonged to her, now that she had found him again.

He kissed her when he left her at for the trolley stop, but he didn't offer to accompany her home. However, he did make her promise to return the next day. Clara wondered why Carlos had seemed so distant to her; most likely, the story of his wife's death had upset her.

III

*S*he began to discover signs of good fortune, to which she was unaccustomed, in everything. The night before, she had arrived at the apartment just ahead of Victor, with enough time to get undressed and pretend to be asleep; that very morning he had told her he needed to take the afternoon train to Rosario, where he'd remain for three days. Clara pretended to be worried because he hadn't warned her far enough in advance for her to send his suit to the dry cleaner, but she had to restrain herself from singing while she cleaned his tie and ironed his pants. Then she accompanied him to the station to be sure he wouldn't miss the 2:37. To pay her back for her solicitousness, Victor bought her a chocolate bar with peanuts. Clara stuck it in her purse, and once the train had pulled away, she hopped on the subway in order to savor it in the peace and quiet of her home while she thought about Carlos.

The night before had been too complicated to reconstruct in detail, but she still felt a sensation of inexplicable hatred and fear towards that Monona woman. So much thinking could make anyone ugly – better rest a bit so I'll look prettier than the rich lady.

At six o'clock sharp she arrived at the main entrance of Parque Retiro. Carlos was already waiting for her there, and that single detail made her imagine that everything would be different from what she had known until then.

They went inside. Carlos put his arm around her shoulders, saying, "The park is yours. We can go wherever you like." And Clara greedily eyed all those rides turning in circles and weaving in and out and running all around her. "Let's go on that one! No, that other one! Oh! The Caterpillar, the Hammer – how lovely! I'm going to get so dizzy!"

Carlos had a ticket book for twelve different rides. Clara was beside herself with joy. He kissed her every time the ferris wheel reached the top, just as she had asked him to do. When they got off, they ran hand in hand to another ride that whirled around at full speed and knocked them, laughing, against each other. The most exciting one was the train that entered a dark tunnel, only to plunge suddenly into the water. They embraced, frightened, happy, and drenched in laughter. They didn't try the Hammer because they would have had to separate and sit opposite each other, and they wanted to stay together always, even if it had to be upside down.

From the roller coaster they could see the masts of the ships in the port. Clara was about to cry out with excitement, but she contained herself in time, remembering the confession he had made to her the night before in that same place: you can never take too many precautions to hold on to happiness. A single word, an out-of-place gesture, can destroy it forever. She was determined to preserve it now that she had found it, and for that reason she had to attend to every detail with a mother's vigilant eye.

They were breathless with enthusiasm and fatigue, and they still had four tickets left when Carlos realized he had to hurry and get ready to sing. As they ran hand in hand, he shouted, "Try to hide so Monona won't see you. Otherwise she'll make a fuss about what happened yesterday."

Carlos turned around to go in through the artists' entrance, and Clara slipped into a dimly lit corner. After just a little while, she noticed Monona dancing among a group of men.

Minutes later they announced Carlos, and Clara changed her position so she could see him more clearly: he seemed better looking than ever now that she was sure she loved him, and he looked over to the side as though he could find her in the darkness. When he began to sing, Clara regretted not having watched Monona more carefully: what would become of her if Monona showed up just then and started talking and talking, if it all started up again and she couldn't listen to her Carlos. Luckily, she located her again on the dance floor, dancing up close with a tall, skinny man. That must be Cacho, and she felt relieved because the other woman was very busy.

A man with a thin mustache approached and asked her to dance. I can't, but thanks anyway. I'm waiting for my boyfriend... And she was glad she hadn't presented her pink card, glad she hadn't ordered the cocktail with that ill-fated kumquat, glad no one could force her to dance. When the waiter came over, she ordered an orange soda.

Meanwhile, Carlos was attacking a milonga that spoke of love. Clara wasn't familiar with it, but she was sure he had chosen it especially for her. Carlos's voice, which she heard through a loudspeaker right behind her head, was lulling her to sleep when suddenly she spied Monona there, a few steps away, allowing a man to kiss her on the neck in a position Clara thought was unseemly and uncomfortable.

She wanted to point out to her that the strap of her dress had fallen down and you could see her bra, and when she stretched backwards, her skirt, which was too narrow, rose above her knee. She might have given her some kind of sign because at that moment, Monona lifted her head, pulling away from the man's lips, and suddenly she was sitting there demurely at her own table. She gave her a wink of recognition, gently pushing her companion away.

Before the song was over, Monona had already abandoned the other guy and was sitting opposite Clara.

"They tricked me! Do you realize that? Those pigs tricked me! I'll make them pay for it. Who do they think they are? We'll see who's the sharpest one around here. Go on, tell me exactly what the guy looked like yesterday, the one who told you Cacho was looking for me."

"Why?" Clara asked, with the most innocent expression.

"Because Cacho wasn't looking for me at all, dummy! He was at his place with the redhead, the one from the cabaret. And I had to go show up there... Shit! I felt like such a jerk!"

"You don't know Cacho, so you can't understand this. Most of the guys around here are jealous of him and would do anything to screw him up. That's why they told me to go there, 'cause they knew he was with the gringa, all right. You've gotta help me; we'll make that bastard pay. As soon as you see him, you point him out to me. I'll go and tell Cacho. He doesn't fool around with this stuff, even though we ended up laughing about it. But he doesn't fool around with this stuff. Anway, he's not vengeful, that's for sure: he promised to take me to Mar del Plata this weekend if I behave myself..."

She leaped up and disappeared. Clara remained pondering her last words and didn't listen to Carlos singing *Mano a Mano*. It would be worth it to see the blue-green sea topped with foam. I wonder what Monona has do to get him to take her to the sea? When I was a kid, behaving myself meant helping mama mop the floor, washing the dishes, and also going to Mass on Sunday. And later, behaving myself meant not letting the boys kiss me on dark streets and stopping them when they pawed me. What the hell could behaving yourself mean now? I'm going to look for Monona and ask.

Monona was dancing with the same partner as before, but when she saw Clara, she left him there and ran over to her.

"Hey, didja see that guy?"

"No, but I wanted to talk to you for a minute..."

"Okay, I'll tell Slim over there to wait for me. Play a little hard-to-get. Gimme a break!"

She returned, quite upset: "Okay, spit it out. What's eatin' you?"

"I just wanted to know how you have to behave in order to get Cacho to take you to Mar del Plata."

"I have to bring him at least three big ones, of course."

"Three thousand pesos! Do you need that much to see the sea?"

"What the fuck sea are you talkin' about? What we wanna see is the bread on the water, not the sea! We play roulette, we gamble, you understand what I'm talkin' about?"

"Roulette? And you never see the sea?"

"Yeah, from the window in the casino, sometimes. But we don't even have time for that. As soon as they open, we're there. They have to throw us out at closing time. And then we sleep till the next day. Cacho puts on a real show when he plays. And he don't wanna waste a minute. You should see him... even when he loses, he plays with such nerve, you'd think he was winnin'. And then he takes it out on me in the hotel, but what the hell do I care? Because sometimes he wins, and then we come back like kings, on a train that takes only four hours. But win or lose, it's always a weekend we spend together. You think that's a lot, three big ones?"

How can there be people who go to the sea without seeing it? Maybe Cacho is so great that if you're with him, nothing else matters. But I don't think there's anything more important than the sea. If there is, I'd really like to meet a man like Cacho.

She needed someone who could make her forget everything she had experienced up till now. Not someone dominant like Cacho, but rather calm and very wise, a man on whom she could rely completely. Powerful, yes, like the sea, and a little bit mysterious. She wished she could find out if some day she'd meet a man like that, so different from the others she'd known so far... She thought about someone strong who would protect her, and she felt very sorry for herself for always having met people as weak as she was. Even Carlos, who seemed to be so strong, had allowed himself to be dominated by his wife.

Meanwhile, Monona kept on talking about Cacho, but she already knew how not to listen, and with a sigh, she uttered aloud a phrase she had heard her mother repeat: "What will become of us women now that there are no more real men around!"

At that moment, however, she saw Carlos approaching, and she regretted having harbored so many unpleasant thoughts, forgetting the

happy times they had spent together. She told herself she was a fool
to want to search for new dreams now that her old ones had become
a reality.

Carlos looked at Clara very tenderly, but his tenderness was gone
as he turned to Monona: "You, here?"

"Yeah, I'm here, I'm here. You know me well enough not to be
surprised to see me, right? I was telling your little friend here that no
one puts anything over on Cacho."

"Oh, Cacho."

"Yeah, Cacho. If jealousy was catching…'cause when they ask
him to sing, he sings better than some people who call themselves
singers. But he don't care… he's Mr. Modest."

"Hey, Massetti!" she shouted to a boy at the opposite table. "Tell
me if I'm lyin' when I say Cacho sings great!"

"Terrific," the boy replied, rolling his eyes.

"See? See? What'd I tell you?"

"Nobody said Cacho couldn't sing," and Carlos fidgeted in
his chair.

"Well, at least you recognize it. And tell me, what'd you do with
that rich old bag, if you don't mind my asking? What'd you do?"

"I sent her packing, for your information."

"A great sacrifice, huh?"

"Nothing of the sort – for Clara, I'd do that and much more. The
other woman took it very hard, though."

"Sure, sure, for losing you. Get outta here; you're such a brag-
gart. But now I've gotta split 'cause he's waitin' for me, and I don't
wanna leave him hangin'."

They got up and left, also. They left Parque Retiro behind, walking slowly toward the trolley.

"Listen, Clarita, I don't want you to see that Monona any more.
She's trash, bad company for you. Tomorrow, while I'm singing, wait
for me outside so you don't have to hang around all those lowlifes,
okay?"

Clara didn't reply. As she plodded up Plaza San Martín, she
thought that Carlos was a wonderful man, too, and she hadn't appreciated him enough. Abandoning that rich woman for her, a plain girl like
her. Just thinking about it made her tingle inside and feel like laughing. A woman loaded with jewels, with diamonds! And he had had the
strength to say no to her, to tell her he'd never see her again. Carlos

was a real man, the kind who knows what he wants. With his wife out of the way, he would be capable of making a thousand sacrifices for her.

She pressed herself against Carlos, and he kissed her in the shade of one of the trees in the plaza.

"Don't you want to come with me tonight?"

But she was determined to play hard-to-get, like Monona, now that she had conquered a man.

"I can't. I'm living with a very strict aunt now. She'll be frightened if I get home too late."

"How about tomorrow?"

"We'll see…"

"What time should we meet?"

"Umm… at seven, like today."

"That's so late!"

"You have to be patient."

"But it's true you love me, isn't it, Clarita?"

"Yes," she replied, and she buried her face in his shoulder, shyly.

One question was still burning in her mouth. She decided to ask it just before hopping up onto the trolley that was waiting at the station: "Aren't you sorry you left that rich lady?"

"Come on, Clara, don't give me that crap. Don't you realize that the business about the rich lady was all made up?"

IV

*T*hat's what's wrong with dreams: they make you feel better when you're sad, but when you're happy, they're annoying. There are no limits in dreams, but in life there are, and what a girl imagined to be perfect turns out to have a lot of weak points, factory defects or something like that.

Carlos is good, and he loves me, but Victor loves me, too; if he didn't, he wouldn't have sent me this pretty postcard all in color with lovers on it and silvery sparkles. Each one loves me in his own way and from his own standpoint, but neither of them is capable of loving me totally and unconditionally, the way it should be.

She got up earlier than usual despite her fatigue, and without even eating breakfast, she began to sew the dress she had cut out the week before. She didn't want to disappoint Carlos; it's enough to have one disillusioned lover in a relationship. He could still hang on to all his illusions when he saw her in her flowered dress, so stylish. She had to leave the sleeves off at the last minute in order to make her date on time. She decided to add them later on, in autumn.

She looked at herself in the mirror and felt satisfied with her work.

"It doesn't matter," she said to her reflection. "The disappointment won't last long. As soon as I forget about the Carlos I dreamed of, the real one will win out."

She left too late, so she had to run the five blocks to the bus stop. Then she arrived at Parque Retiro all out of breath, about forty-five minutes late.

Carlos greeted her with a frown: "I've been waiting for you for an hour."

"And I've got a new dress…" Clara said, spinning around on her heels.

"Now we'll have to hurry, or I'll be late." He took her arm and pulled her towards the corner.

"Where are we going?" Clara shouted, surprised by his brusqueness.

"You'll see."

"Aren't we going to the rides?"

"Not today."

"But you still have some tickets left."

Carlos wasn't listening to her. He yelled "Taxi!" and pushed her into the car. Clara, disappointed and sat down without worrying about straightening out her skirt, which would surely wrinkle. Nothing mattered any more because she wasn't going to fly through the air, swelling like a balloon.

In the rooms-by-the-hour hotel she had to take off her dress, and in his frenzy, Carlos pulled apart a loose stitch. The dress, forgotten, was cast thoughtlessly over a chair, together with Clara's former enthusiasm for Carlos.

As he had clearly stated, he was in a hurry, and on the way back to Parque Retiro, he recommended: "I'd rather you didn't go to the Palace tonight while I'm singing. Wait for me outside. I'll give you the tickets to go on the rides."

"Don't you want me to hear you sing?"

"No, you make me nervous. Besides, I don't like it at all when you run around with that witch, Monona. She's the worst sort; she'll put all kinds of ideas into your head. And let's not even talk about Cacho and his gang. You know Cacho?"

"No."

"It's better you don't. Promise me you won't come."

"I promise." She shrugged her shoulders.

Promises are made to be kept, even if you feel all kinds of sadness weighing on your shoulders. The time they had spent in the rooms-by-the-hour hotel had left a unpleasant taste in her mouth and a hole in the pit of her stomach, like when she drank too much. With drinking, it was understandable because she wasn't accustomed to alcohol, while the other thing… Of course, with Carlos, she had wanted it to be completely different, and yet it seemed so very much the same…

Clara felt more alone than ever at that moment, since loneliness weighs more heavily when there's someone else involved. When there's no one else, loneliness isn't heavy; it keeps you company.

She wandered around, indifferent to the colored lights, and she wished it were Monday or Tuesday night, when Carlos went on later, but it was Thursday. There was quite a big audience, and Carlos had to hurry to give the floor to the other tango orchestra, the one with four bandoneones. She wouldn't have felt so alone if it had been the dead of night, but twilight has been known to causing feelings of abandonment for more than one person.

In a gesture of self-preservation, she went up to one of the kiosks where they sold cookies and sandwiches and bought a bologna sandwich wrapped in plastic. Her distress made her hungry. At least the sandwich would be a distraction. She nibbled as she walked over to a brightly colored tent, and passing by a group of boys, she heard them call out to her:

"Is that delicious, baby?"

"How about a little piece for me?"

"Come here, sweetie, I want to smell the flowers on your blouse..."

But she kept on walking, although they seemed nice. Maybe they attended Gaeta Academy, where the art of giving compliments, with all its rules, was taught.

At last she entered the colored tent, where the barker was shouting, megaphone in hand: "Step right up, ladies and gentlemen, step right up if you want to learn what the stars have in store for you. Don't wait a moment longer; your future is right here in the hands of this swami, just arrived from ancient India. Step right up, ladies and gentlemen, no pushing."

Two soldiers, each with a girl on his arm, drew closer, then another man, then a fat lady with a little boy carrying a balloon. Clara drew near, also, and on top of the pedestal she saw a young man, sitting with crossed arms and legs. Meanwhile, the barker stood there, extolling the merits of the swami-just-arrived-from-ancient-India, who sat motionless, flashes of light shooting from the enormous ruby mounted in his turban.

Clara was so close to the Hindu that she could have touched his shiny, wide black satin pants. His long, fine hands fascinated her. She raised her eyes to look at him straight on and discovered an impassive face with very deep-set gray eyes. She surmised that the man up there, so far beyond her reach, was even more alone than she, like a rock in the middle of a blue, twilit sea. But instead of feeling lonely like her, he was indifferent to the rest of society, and he didn't feel hunger, thirst, or even melancholy. She would have liked to touch him thoroughly and catch his remoteness, but she didn't even dare hold out a peso so the magician could predict her future. The lady with the little boy, who was fat and much less romantic than Clara, paid her money, emitting little bursts of repressed laughter under the serious gaze of her son, who appeared to be judging her harshly.

The man in the turban took a cylinder and with deliberate, almost liturgical movements, spilled a powder inside that created a spark. Then red and blue smoke escaped from the cylinder, turning him into angel and devil alternately. When the smoke died, he placed his hand inside the cylinder and extracted a small piece of paper, which he handed to the fat lady. The boy, who had stood there with his mouth agape, resumed his expression of hostile superiority.

Clara was the only one who couldn't get over her astonishment: she kept staring at that impassive figure. The fat lady tried to read by the dwindling light inside the tent, and Clara thought that she would like to have that man hand over her fortune with his long, dark hands. She stood there staring up at him for a long time however, before she could make up her mind to rummage through her purse in search of the peso which would purchase her future.

The barker never stopped shouting, and she handed him her ticket timidly, uncertain whether or not to interrupt him. From atop his pedestal, the man in the turban looked at her out of the corner of his eye, but she didn't notice.

The puffs of red and blue smoke were even brighter for Clara than they had been for the fat lady, and the Hindu balanced the cylinder so they would fly higher. When she saw the little piece of paper, Clara felt a tingling run down her spine, and when the Hindu handed it to her, she tried to touch his fingers, but he didn't even blink. He was too high up.

What marvelously powerful indifference! I'll have to keep this yellow paper safe in the bottom of my purse. It must be good to carry your destiny around with you, even though it might be awful to find out what it says. I know that everything in life is set beforehand, and wanting to know your future is like going forward too fast and running the risk of reaching the end ahead of time. I'm not afraid of death because it's far off, but I don't plan to do anything to tempt it or make it notice me.

The two brash soldiers had received their respective fortunes and were reading them aloud, guffawing. She wanted to warn them, make them be quiet, too, because she didn't like the way they refused to take her Hindu seriously. Still, despite their laughter, the Hindu remained unaffected, arms and legs crossed, on top of his pedestal, not moving a single muscle, as if he were far above human affairs.

The barker's screechy voice annoyed Clara. Spectators came and went around him, and the group continually changed in appearance. She was the only one who didn't have the strength to drag herself away from that place; by way of justification, she held out another peso and received another little piece of paper.

It's violet. I have two destinies, like supernatural beings. I'm going to keep the two pieces of paper very carefully in the bottom of my purse so they won't feel lonely. Even arithmetic can make mistakes, because if you add one loneliness to another loneliness, instead of making a bigger loneliness, they cancel each other out and keep each other company.

The Hindu never stopped looking at her out of the corner of his eye, but she felt he was so remote that she didn't even worry about being noticed. She did observe some bystanders looking at her intently, and to avoid giving them reason to do so, she picked up her change purse and counted her coins until they made up a peso's worth, which she handed over to the announcer. The Hindu took his cylinder and repeated the angel-devil trick. Clara watched him with wide-open eyes, just as the fat lady's son had done; it was better than going to the movies to see the same picture three times in a row, because here the central character was made of flesh and blood, and the story was placed into her own hands. That way the secret would remain between the two of them, without anyone else's having even the smallest role.

She had three destinies now. Perhaps she could even choose among them. She would have liked to ask the Hindu, although he probably didn't know the language she spoke.

Three destinies, and I'm going to have to choose without seeing what they are. She stuck her hand into her purse and picked out one at random. It's the red one, the last one, the shiniest. And also the most dangerous. Red, a color that suits me.

She was happy. She had chosen her path freely.

V

Carlos begged her to spend the night with him because he needed her. Clara didn't feel like being needed. She felt like needing. She got angry and left him standing at the exit of Parque Retiro.

The next morning, when she awoke, she felt responsible for her newly chosen destiny, with a mission to accomplish: she would remain at home, expectantly, without making any decisions. It was Friday. Victor had told her he would be back on Saturday. By afternoon, she began to feel quite lonely and filled with remorse towards poor Carlos, whom she had abandoned like an old rag, without any explanation. She had no right to do a thing like that, after all. She tried waxing the floor as a distraction, but she was so nervous she kept bumping into the furniture. She tried to iron, but every so often, she put the iron aside and walked back and forth in the room liked a caged animal. Whenever she closed her eyes, she saw that man's face appear behind a curtain of smoke; her head ached; she felt dizzy. She undressed and stood under the shower; even that didn't calm her. She decided to wait until nightfall and return to Parque Retiro.

She quickly paid for her ticket and headed toward the Hindu's tent, but between the Caterpillar and the Haunted Train, she spied the yellowish glow of the Dance Palace and felt an enormous weight in her heart. She decided to go and ask Carlos's forgiveness and explain to him how she had chosen a different destiny.

It was too early, and there were very few people in the ballroom. She covered it from one end to the other, zigzagging between the tables. As she passed in front of the musicians' platform, she extended her hand as if to bid him goodbye. Sadly, she recalled the emotion she had felt on seeing Carlos again. It's a pity; those feelings that make your legs tremble and your throat catch don't last very long, and then they leave a hole that's very hard to fill. She hesitated for a moment, once again imagining him beneath the spotlights that made him look bigger and more imposing, when she heard a voice behind her.

"Are you waiting for that loser? You messed up – he's on later tonight."

She took her by the arm, guiding her towards a group of people who were sitting at a table in back. Clara was afraid that Monona would try to steal her new red fortune, and she roughly jerked away the hand that was holding on to her and ran out of the room, before the other woman's astonished gaze.

She ran among the ball-toss stands, passed quickly by the test-your-skill booths and the kiosk where she had bought the bologna sandwich the day before. She stopped only long enough to enter the Hindu's multicolored tent, although when she raised her eyes, the only thing she found was a dark curtain covering the upper portion of the pedestal.

She could barely think or breathe, or even move. She decided to unfold the little red slip of paper which she carried in her purse to find out what to do next, but fear of bad luck held her back. The best thing to do when you don't know what to do is wait, so she sat down in the entrance of a closed kiosk opposite the tent. You mustn't try to hurry things along, and, resting her elbow on her knee, she put her chin in her hand, tracing little circles in the dust with her left foot. She saw some other feet passing by, but she didn't lift her gaze even when those feet, which were wearing very misshapen brown shoes, came closer. The man's shoes stopped just a few steps away from her, and a slightly ironic voice asked:

"Waiting for someone?"

Clara thought that this was going to be a replay, just as when she had run into Monona. Raising her eyes, she saw the white shirt and coffee-colored face with its aquiline nose, and she realized that this time was different, because he was exactly the one she had been waiting for. As she hadn't thought of anything to explain her presence there, she opened her purse, removing one of the one-peso bills that she had specially prepared before leaving her house.

"Tell my fortune," she explained in a tiny voice, handing him the money."

"Keep that; it's on me today. Come have a coffee with me."

They went to the café, which had outdoor metal tables, over which planes flew in monotonous circles.

"I thought you didn't speak Spanish," she said, just to say something, and he understood enough not to laugh at her.

"The truth is I'm a one hundred percent native of Buenos Aires, but I know all about Hindu secrets just as if I had been there."

"Is that true? That really is funny. How do you predict the future?"

"It takes a little bit of magic… Give me your left hand…"

Clara hid her hands behind her back: "No, no, no! I've chosen my destiny myself, but I don't want to find out."

"Whatever you say, but I'm sure you must have a very beautiful heart line."

"Oh, sure!" Clara sighed sadly.

"I'm never wrong." He brought his chair over next to Clara's. "So, you've already chosen your destiny?"

"Yeah, the red one."

"Then you'll have to watch out for bulls."

"It's not animals I'm afraid of. I'm afraid of men."

"Same thing."

"You think so? And women?"

"I don't want to offend you. I'd rather you asked me some other kind of question."

"If you only knew how much it takes to offend me these days!"

He stared at her intently, and after a long while, said in a quiet voice, like a confession: "I saw you yesterday. You stood outside my tent for almost an hour. Why?"

"I don't know. I liked that little machine that gave off smoke…"

"That isn't true!" He squeezed her arm furiously.

"If you know better than me, why ask?"

They regarded each other defiantly. Suddenly he came closer and kissed her on the lips.

"That's why," he replied, sitting down again with a sigh of relief. "But let's talk about you. Tell me about your life," he added, after lighting a cigarette.

Clara once more discovered in him the indifference of the previous evening, and her admiration for him came flooding back.

"There's nothing worthwhile about my life, nothing to tell. Until recently, my name was Clara, but since I was told it doesn't suit me, I'm going to have to change names. Which one do you like?"

"Clara."

"But that's the same one…"

"No, it's not the same. Before, you were anybody's Clara. Now, ever since you said your name, you're my Clara."

"And your name is Swam… what?"

"That's my name for other people. For you, I'm Alejandro."

"Alejandro…" Clara repeated, almost to herself.

"What are you doing tonight?"

"Nothing."

"And tomorrow? And the next day? And every day?"

"Nothing, nothing, nothing. I had a job, but I gave it up."

"You should never give up a job. Then you go around kind of lost. I wanted to be an architect, but I couldn't finish my studies."

She felt sorry for him, just like Doña Ramona's son. He came to the capital to become a doctor, but after just one year, he had to go back to his town to plant carrots like his father.

"Going to school is so expensive..."

"It wasn't because of the expense. I had a scholarship. But I had a fight with a professor in one of those student protests, and I broke his nose. They expelled me; afterwards, I couldn't get back to my books. Now I pull rabbits out of hats; I read minds. I'm a magician. I can also read a deck of cards. If you come to my house, I'll show you all the tricks you want."

Clara's eyes were shining, but common sense triumphed.

"You have to work now."

"This is no kind of work for me... they can all go to hell! I'll straighten it out right now... Hey, kid!"

He summoned a boy who was walking by and gave him five pesos.

"Here, take this. Tell the guy who announces the act at the Hindu's tent (you know which one? next to the bumper cars)... tell that man the Hindu got sick all of a sudden and he went home. But be sure to tell him, okay? Or the next time I see you, I'll kick the shit out of you."

"Yes, sir!" the boy replied, running off.

"But the other man will get angry with you."

"Let him get angry if he wants. I'm fed up with all this."

VI

The number 303 bus arrived at the terminal, and the few remaining passengers exited slowly. Alejandro led Clara to the banks of the Riachuelo, and she laughed enthusiastically at the brightly-painted houses.

"How pretty, Alejandro, look, how lovely!"

"What do you mean, lovely? It's an eyesore; it's seedy. Come on, come on, don't waste time here."

"Do you live in a colored house like those?"

"God forbid. I hate bright colors."

Clara concluded that his experiences as an architecture student must have made him want to appear severe, so she didn't insist.

They reached a house, several stories high, with zinc patches on the walls. You had to climb down thirteen steps to enter. Clara counted them.

There were some children fighting on the patio, and their mothers shouted at them to come inside and eat. Clara and Alejandro climbed up a rickety staircase where fumes and odors from all the kitchens blended together. Clara felt nauseated and leaned on Alejandro's arm. On the first floor, a baby was crying with all the vigor his new lungs could muster. On the second floor, an old man was coughing, a woman was singing, and seven or eight men were arguing in the hallway. All those confused, intermingled noises came together on the third floor.

Alejandro lived on the third floor. The door to his room was standing open.

"Aren't you afraid of being robbed?" Clara asked.

"Robbed of what?"

Inside, shoved into a corner, the wide bed stood unmade; it rested on a pile of books, looking round and warm, like a laying hen. On one side of the window was an enormous table covered with papers and rulers, and beyond that was a wash basin with a dilapidated mirror above it and a shelf covered with brushes and tubes of paint. A curtain concealed a corner that served as a wardrobe. A few books on the floor, an old armchair with its stuffing falling out, and a straight chair completed the suite.

Alejandro looked at her proudly. "Bohemian life," he said, and she believed him.

Since he didn't have a key, Alejandro dragged some weights out from under the bed, placing them against the closed door.

"They weigh two hundred pounds; I don't think anyone will be able to move them."

Then he went over to Clara to kiss her, but skirted slightly around her and headed for the table, removing a package of water biscuits from the drawer along with a few slices of boiled ham wrapped in a piece of greasy paper.

"Here, eat. I don't have any butter because it melts in this heat."

He pulled out a bottle of wine from underneath the bed and went to the bathroom to rinse out his only glass.

"Sit down," he told Clara, pointing to the bed. He handed her the glass of wine.

Clara sat down and ate as if she were in her own house, although she had never seen such a strange house as this before. She glanced over the book titles without understanding them. On the cover of one of them, she saw the palm of a hand, crisscrossed with many lines and some stars. On others, she read *Rituals and Dogma of High Magic, The Golden Bough, Eastern Occultism,* and she told herself that Alejandro must be quite the scholar.

He had seated himself on the bed, watching her look around. When they had finished the ham, he pulled out a basket of cherries from among the papers and popped them into her mouth.

"Hand me the towel," he said, afterwards. "It's over there, beside the pillow."

Clara stretched out on the bed to reach the towel, but she pulled back suddenly with a scream: something warm and hairy stirred among the covers.

"It's nothing; it's just Asmodeus," and he picked up an enormous black cat that looked at him adoringly.

"The perfect magician's indispensable companion," he added, stroking its back. "But you'll have to go now, Asmodeus, because you're frightening the lady."

He went over to the window and yanked it open.

"Go on, go eat some birdies on the roof," and he closed the window again, in spite of the heat. Asmodeus didn't budge, however; he watched from the other side of the glass as his master's steps drew closer to the woman who had usurped his place and he began kissing her.

Asmodeus's green eyes grew wider, not wanting to miss a single detail of that feverish movement, and when the couple finally lay still on the bed, he began to meow desperately because he wanted to participate as well and rub himself against those two naked bodies, placing his head right there where his master's hand was, between the woman's warm, generous breasts, and fall asleep.

He had to stay outside all night long meowing, and he resigned himself merely to watching what transpired within, since the light had been left on.

Clara didn't dare move around in bed, in order not to disturb Alejandro. With her head resting against his shoulder and one leg against his belly, she could comfortably observe his perfectly-muscled body and his aquiline profile. She felt numb, but he had made her happy, and she wanted to thank him somehow.

Alejandro reached out his free hand and grabbed a cigarette, lit it, and began to smoke, moving only his right arm.

Clara thought of his indifference when he was up on the pedestal and tried to imitate him, to become like him, to complete him. Sleep swept over her in waves, but each time she opened her eyes again, she saw him there, always in the same position, unflappable, smoking and staring at the ceiling. She kept trying not to move and, although her face grew taut and she fought against her aching sleepiness, it finally overcame her, and she dozed again for a few minutes.

At dawn she finally managed to emulate him. She no longer felt that unpleasant electricity in her hip and leg. But then someone knocked violently at the door, and she jumped, startled.

"Listen, mister! Can't you hear your damn cat screeching out there like he's dying? He won't let anyone sleep!"

Alejandro didn't budge. His only response was the monotonous movement of the cigarette towards his lips as he replied, "Leave Asmodeus alone, woman. He's probably looking for a she-cat."

"You're the one who runs around with she-cats. And if you don't shut that lousy cat up, I'm gonna call Don Anselmo, the policeman who lives in the basement, and have him shoot it dead."

Alejandro got up, annoyed, went to the window, and opened it noisily.

"Come, Asmodeus," he said.

The cat leaped inside happily, rubbing himself against his master's legs; his master stood in front of the open window, looking at the sky, which had turned orange. Clara took advantage of the opportunity to cover herself with the single blanket in the room, to try to forget about the cold she had felt all night, and the cat's howling. She was falling asleep beneath the warm blanket when Alejandro called her over, and she had to get up and walk to the window just as she was, naked, because he was naked, too, and she didn't want to make him angry.

Alejandro grabbed her by the shoulders, saying: "I've thought it over carefully, and now I've decided. You're going to come and live with me forever. It's too late to refuse now. When a woman spends a whole night with a man, wide awake, without saying a word, she has no right to leave him alone afterwards."

Asmodeus watched her from the armchair. His green eyes glinted with a mixture of admiration and hatred.

VII

*T*he next day, Victor arrived at one p.m., put his suitcase down in the hall, and called for his slippers.

"What a miserable job!" he complained, kissing her on the cheek absent-mindedly. "You have no idea how hot is was in Mercedes. And that train! A bunch of old biddies who didn't stop chattering the whole time. Bring me a bottle of beer, nice and cold. I'm dying of thirst. But I sold two refrigerators. Pretty nice commission, huh? Of course, I had to work like a horse, galloping back and forth in the middle of the afternoon, and it was as hot as hell. But I'll finally be able to buy myself that blue poplin suit I saw the other day. I know, I know! Don't interrupt me. You want your blender; women always try to avoid the puny little bit of work they have to do. Next time, okay? And don't interrupt me – I'm telling you, it won't do you any good to insist. A traveling salesman has to be well dressed, and that suit is exactly what I need for this time of year. I'm dying of the heat in my serge one. On the way over, I met a guy named Menéndez who said he loved his poplin suit. Imagine, you can wash it out at home and everything. Do you realize how much we'll save in dry cleaning bills? Great guy, Menéndez, we talked about a lot of things. I've got to go meet him now at two-thirty, at the Paulista Bar on Callao. He's well-connected; he's a salami and sausage salesman. Maybe we'll be able to join forces, because, like he says, you've got to have a good fridge to keep salami fresh. And speaking of salami... I guess lunch is ready, huh?"

Clara nodded.

He laid his jacket and tie on the bed and went into the kitchen.

"Cold chicken with mayonnaise!" he exclaimed, rubbing his hands together. "My favorite."

He sat down at the table and cut off almost half the chicken for himself. Clara sliced off a wing and put it on her plate, taking a teaspoonful of mayonnaise.

Victor helped himself to everything that was left and wiped his plate with a piece of bread.

They had finished eating when he deigned to glance at Clara.

"Hey, you don't look so good. You're all pale, and you've got bags under your eyes. You're not going to tell me you're pregnant, are you?"

"No."

"Thank God! That would be the last straw."

"It's worse than that..."

"Worse? Impossible. Nothing could be worse. You sure you're not pregnant?"

Clara shook her head.

"Well then, woman, don't exaggerate. It must be something trivial..."

"No, it's not trivial. I'm leaving. I'm leaving you."

Victor choked on his words: "You're leaving? Where to? With whom?" He started to cough.

Clara, felt sorry for him and patted him on the back.

"I didn't think you'd care so much. It's just that I'm going," she said, sadly.

"You've lost your mind, woman. I always told myself one day you'd lose your mind. Look, don't do anything rash. You can't leave all this comfort just like that. I've given you a roof over your head, food on the table... Think about me a little and don't make hasty decisions... Now I've got to run because Menéndez is waiting to discuss business with me, but I'm sure when I get back, you'll tell me this was just a joke."

By the time he returned, Clara had already left, taking all her things with her. She had said goodbye to Victor's tidy apartment, and on the nightstand she had left him a note that read simply "Forgive Me" and then "Thank You." She also left him the two pawnshop tickets that she no longer needed, because with Alejandro's wages, she would never be able to recover her watch and her *mate*.

The first three days she spent with Alejandro left an intense flavor of happiness in her mouth. He had arranged things so that his boss, the carnival barker, thought he was sick and couldn't go to Parque Retiro, and in order to justify that excuse somewhat, he spent the daylight hours in bed, getting up at nightfall to walk towards the Riachuelo, climb up to the Avellaneda Bridge to watch the ships, or go to Vuelta de Rocha and simply sit on a bench, without saying a word. When they were hungry, they went to some cheap restaurant and had fried fish and bought bread and sausages for the next day. Sometimes they stopped outside a café to listen to the sounds of a *bandoneón* coming from inside.

A threatening letter from his business partner and the lack of funds for their most basic necessities forced Alejandro out of this peaceful existence. He was getting dressed to leave when Clara reached out for her dress, draped over a chair.

"No. I don't want you to come with me. What are you going to do there, waiting for me for hours on end? Stay here and keep Asmodeus company. There's still a piece of spinach pie left. Eat and go to bed early. I'll be back around one."

He gave her a hurried kiss and disappeared before she could object. Clara peered out the window to watch him cross the patio, but the food odors that wafted up in gusts made her feel like throwing up.

Asmodeus, who had reclaimed his favorite spot at the head of the bed, stared at her furiously. She curled up at the other end, her head resting against the wall and her feet dangling. She didn't want to move or even think. Alejandro doesn't want me to watch him shining through all those mysterious puffs of smoke, like I love to do. When he's here by my side, I always half-close my eyes and imagine him on his pedestal, so far away and safe. And now he won't let me go any more, and he wants me to forget about all that. It doesn't matter – if I close my eyes real tight until they hurt, I can see his face there forever.

In addition to her eyes, the nape of her neck hurt from leaning her head against the wall for so long, but Asmodeus was sleeping peacefully on the pillow and it was better not to wake him so he wouldn't look at her furiously again. There were voices and music coming from Parque Retiro, and she couldn't go, or it would annoy Alejandro. She was allowed only to leave the light on so she wouldn't be afraid of the darkness and the creaking of unfamiliar steps in the hall. She thought of the ships passing below the bridge and of the brightly-hued houses displaying their same happy colors beneath the same lights, but she couldn't summon enough energy to get dressed and descend the three flights to the street now that he had gone.

When Alejandro returned at one-thirty, he found her sleeping at the foot of the bed, with her legs dangling off. The light was still on, and Asmodeus had taken refuge beneath a chair. Alejandro was tired and a bit fed up with things in general, but he tried to lift her and place her in the correct position, with her head on the pillow. In spite of his careful efforts, she opened her eyes and said, unperturbed at seeing him beside her, "You mustn't look behind you…"

Alejandro realized she had been frightened of being alone, and that she hadn't been strong enough to place the weights against the door. He really had to buy a lock or a deadbolt. A deadbolt is a humble, useful thing, unpretentious, but he opened his billfold and realized he didn't even have enough to buy that. He stroked her hair gently so as not to wake her, and told her in a very soft voice that she had to conquer her fear because there was no other solution. He, on the other hand, could work days or change jobs, but he found the very idea of working for money repulsive, and after thinking it over carefully, he berated her for having reminded him of his poverty.

The next morning, the first thing he said was: "Don't let me catch you sleeping with the light on again; after all, I'm the one who pays the electric bills around here."

If you want to avoid complaints, the best thing to do is act furious. He believed in the philosophy of striking first.

Clara woke up early and walked around the apartment without knowing what to do; she tried to straighten out his work table, but he had forbidden her to touch his papers. She tried to sweep but couldn't find a broom; she tried to get washed, but he became enraged because she splashed his books.

"Would you just keep still once and for all! Stop walking around and around like a caged animal."

Asmodeus was sleeping in the armchair, and Clara had to resign herself to going back to bed. She stretched out painstakingly against the wall and waited. At noon, Alejandro deposited his last remaining pesos in her hand and sent her to buy wine, bologna, and bread.

There was quite a long line in front of the bakery, and she took her place there, prepared to wait her turn. The man in front of her turned around and smiled warmly at her.

"I think we've met before, haven't we, miss?"

Clara looked at him indifferently; she had met so many men like him before that she could no longer tell them apart. Besides, she was no good at recognizing faces.

"Of course, we live in the same building," he continued, "on Pedro de Mendoza Street."

"That's right," she replied, biting a hangnail.

"You must be new in this neighborhood. Otherwise you wouldn't be shopping at Bianchi's. Don't think I've been spying on you – no, I just happened to see you come in. But let me assure you, Don Pepe's grocery is much cheaper, even though he doesn't have such a good selection..."

Clara raised her eyebrows.

"You must be surprised to hear me say that," he went on, un-ruffled. "But a bachelor has his habits and knows all the little neighborhood secrets..."

Clara decided to smile; after all, he was very friendly to her. When his turn came, he said, "After you," and let her go first. She timidly asked for a large baguette, and he quickly bought three country loaves. He followed her out, remarking, "Look here, if you want a baguette, you'd better come back in fifteen minutes; they'll be taking out a fresh batch, nice and hot from the oven."

"How well you know your way around here!"

"Well, you know, in my profession you have to keep your eyes wide open..."

"Oh..."

"But we've been talking so much, and we haven't even introduced ourselves. Anselmo Romero, at your service."

He stood at attention and held out his hand.

"Clara Hernández," she said, and she realized how infrequently she had pronounced her last name in the last few years. At least that afforded her a certain amount of dignity.

"I don't want to get you into trouble. I'll go inside first; you follow by yourself. Some of the neighbors have very loose tongues... Just remember, Señorita Clara, if you need anything, Don Anselmo is at your service."

He stepped up his pace to arrive at the tenement ahead of her. Clara thought to herself that she had heard Don Anselmo's name mentioned somewhere...

By the time siesta had ended, she had already forgotten about her recent encounter, and she asked Alejandro to do his act just for her: she wanted to find out if he was an angel or a devil. He became indignant. He was reading about the Cathars and thinking, as they did, that hell could be found in this world. He thought himself capable of plumbing the depths of mysticism, of attaining some kind of truth and redeeming himself, and this woman was forcing him to return to reality, to that simple-minded magic that had nothing to do with Magic, to his tawdry job, so painful for someone like him, who could qualify as an initiate. And so he lost his patience.

"You think I'm in the mood for foolishness? Don't ask for stupid things, and pass me the wine. I'm thirsty."

That night Clara had to exercise all her courage to fall asleep in the dark. She though she heard mysterious noises, and Asmodeus' eyes shone like lights. She got up to give him a little milk and make him think she liked him, but all she could find were two empty wine bottles. She turned out the light, lay down again, told herself that under that roof she had a friend named Don Anselmo. She finally fell asleep, repeating the names of those people who had been kind to her.

Alejandro returned at dawn. He stood there for a long time, staring at her and thinking about his own frustrations, taking perverse pleasure in his failures. He saw himself touching bottom in that tenement in La Boca, sharing his quarters with a prostitute, and he felt happy in his own way. His parents' house in the Belgrano district, the prize for the best neighborhood development project, Inés who had broken off their engagement when he was thrown out of school, the day he left home to forge a new path for himself – it all seemed so far away. Little by little, things had turned out badly for him, and if failure was his destiny, he was prepared to fail until the very end, to fail all the way with nothing half-hearted about it. He thought of the Marquis de Sade, of Giles de Rais, and of the possibility of torturing others physically in order to find oneself. Sitting at Clara's feet, he decided that it was just too much effort, and finally he awakened her to make love, since after all he wasn't providing her bed and board for nothing.

VIII

*A*lejandro had forbidden her to have anything to do with the neighbors, but after spending five mornings lying in bed watching the dust gather, she couldn't stand it any more and asked the woman in number 19, who regarded her suspiciously, if she could borrow a broom. But when she realized that Clara was the one who was living with that oddball up in the garret, she lent her the broom just like that, even offering her the dustpan and feather duster without being asked.

"That guy upstairs may be unfriendly, but he's not bad... and that woman of his looks kind of dumb. But you'll see – she'll return all that stuff to me exactly as I gave it to her, don't worry. She was very pleasant."

In effect, Clara had forced herself to be as pleasant as possible. She said excuse me and thank you, and she promised to return everything in half an hour. That day she felt much lonelier than usual, and she needed some distraction. In the morning Don Anselmo had mentioned to her that next week they wouldn't be able to do their shopping together.

"I've got the morning shift," he explained. "Of course, I can't complain, it's a good location, quiet. You don't have to direct traffic, and those six hours just fly by."

That business of directing traffic caught Clara's attention, and suddenly the little warning bell inside her head started to go off like crazy. She remembered the first night she spent with Alejandro, when the woman who was screaming about Asmodeus had said, "Don Anselmo, the policeman..." So that was it. She couldn't be friends with a policeman on account of her past history, and yet, she needed a friend so badly... Alejandro was sullen and terse, which wasn't an altogether unattractive quality, and might even be considered to constitute ninety percent of his charm, but she had lived with Victor too long to tolerate such a sudden, radical change. Besides, everything that surrounded Alejandro was hostile, like Asmodeus. His belongings didn't like her and fell apart in her hands whenever she needed them most.

First the bathroom faucet, which leaked with an infuriating drip, splashing everything. Then the switch on the nightstand lamp: it was impossible to turn on the night light when she heard steps in the hall. And the heater, too, which gave out a completely useless, little yellow flame. All of it while Alejandro was away, and as soon as he returned, a simple touch of his fingers was enough to return the objects to their normal state.

She began to suspect that he might really be a magician, although she knew very well that real magicians didn't exist, only fake magicians who pulled rabbits from hats and colored handkerchiefs from people's pockets. But in spite of everything, Alejandro had the same power over her as he did over objects, and when he caressed her, he did it so well that she couldn't refuse him anything. Unfortunately, he didn't caress her too often, and sometimes he spent an entire day without saying anything other than what was absolutely necessary:

"Go to the grocery store; hand me the bottle; open up the window for Asmodeus and give him some scraps," and Clara stood there admiring him because he had a perfect profile and he could spend countless hours without moving or sleeping, immersed in his own dark thoughts.

Clara needed to speak with someone once in a while, to unburden herself; that's why she had chatted with Don Anselmo who, as he himself had assured her, was a perfect gentleman. And that's why she asked to borrow the neighbor's broom, more out of a need for human warmth than because of any compulsion to clean. Nonetheless, she concentrated on sweeping in the corners and under the bed as well as she could without unduly disturbing the books piled up on the floor. She cleaned thoroughly, she straightened up carefully, and she even added a saucy touch by spreading her green shawl over the shabby chair. Then she descended the stairs two at a time in order to return the broom before her neighbor could get angry with her and refuse to speak to her again.

She knocked at the door and waited. She was greatly disappointed when two children appeared, but as she didn't know what else to do, she asked for their mother and gave the broom and feather duster to the older one, who must have been about ten years old. The youngster seemed offended and handed the objects over to his little sister.

"This is women's stuff," he said, and then added, trying to make his voice sound deeper and standing on tiptoe: "Um, listen, would you by any chance have a pack of cigarettes for me?"

Clara replied indignantly, "Kids don't smoke!"

"What d'ya mean, smoke! When we wanna do that, we snitch the butts off our old man. He smokes unfiltered, the good stuff. What I want are packs of the other kind, the faggoty kind, the ones that come with silver paper."

And he added, lowering his voice in embarrassment: "They're for decorating the Christmas tree."

Clara allowed herself to become excited. "A Christmas tree! How nice! And where are you planning to put it?"

The boy lowered his head. "Look," he explained, "I don't believe in that stupid junk. I don't fall for that stuff any more. I'm doing it to keep from getting bored, and besides, there'll probably be firecrackers."

Clara's face lit up: "And if I get you a lot of silver paper, will you let me see your tree?"

"Ugh! I just told you it's not mine! We're gonna do it on the patio. Every year old Pocho brings us a big branch of a real pine tree. He's a gardener, y'know? And he plants it for us in a bucket. We have to decorate it with whatever we can find around here. I do it for the kids," he said, pointing to his little brother and sister. "They still believe in it, dumb little guys, and our ma always says they still have time to wise up."

Clara couldn't control herself any longer and she asked, suddenly, gathering all her courage, "Um… couldn't I help you fix up the tree?"

"You gonna bring firecrackers?"

"Well, no… not firecrackers, but I could make little paper dolls."

"Dolls!" the boy muttered scornfully. "If you think that's fun…"

"Sure it's fun! Will you let me?"

"The tree belongs to everybody; on Christmas Eve, even the grownups come downstairs for panettone and cider. The part I like is the cider. I bet I could drink a whole quart without getting smashed. I could even stand on one leg without falling down, an' everything. But if you bring firecrackers, it'll be much better."

"I'll see if I can get you some Roman candles. Do you like them?"

"Great! And go ahead and make the dolls. 'Cause this year the tree's gonna be really big. The guy next door's gonna give us candles; they say he works in a funeral parlor. Look, if you bring the Roman candles, we'll even let you help set up the tree, as a special favor, get it? Me an' the guys like to do stuff on our own. But I'm the boss – if I tell 'em to let you help, they will. But you've gotta bring a lot of dolls and stars and all that junk, you've gotta bring it. And don't forget the Roman candles, okay?"

"Deal."

Clara put her hand out, and the boy shook it with all his might to seal the pact. Then he looked at her triumphantly, saying: "They call me Chichón, 'cause I'm always goin' around with bruises. What's your name?"

"Clara."

"Don't you have a nickname?"

"No."

"Well, don't worry about it, we'll find you one."

When Christmas Eve was only four days away, Clara realized that it was impossible to save up, because Alejandro spent money as soon as he earned it. On good days, he took her to the café, and on bad days they hardly had even a can of mackerel to eat. She was already tired of mackerel, and she hadn't managed to save a single peso to buy the Roman candles. Alejandro had become more taciturn than ever and spoke to her as little as possible.

He spent his time reading his old books filled with strange glyphs and trying to penetrate the secrets of the Cabala. Sometimes he got excited and started to pace in circles, sweating, or else he drew mystical symbols on the wall with charcoal. The room was beginning to take on a sinister air for Clara, and at times he would laugh for no apparent reason. Later, he would remain still for hours on end, and she didn't know how to go about asking him for the few pesos she needed.

One morning as she observed him in profile, admiring his features and his usual indifference, she realized that what she wanted most was for the moment of his departure to arrive. The idea surprised her because it was a new one. In general she hated that moment when he put on his jacket and kissed her goodbye; the night seemed endless because she was alone, and Asmodeus's company gave her chills. But that morning she knew beforehand that she wouldn't waste the night trying to catch a few winks of that sleep which slipped away through her eyelids because Don Anselmo had loaned her some lovely, sharp, curved scissors, and she had already managed to collect enough silver paper to make a whole sky full of stars. Strong, round pieces that she had spread out very carefully from the neck of the wine bottles Alejandro emptied. She had to pull them off before she got to the apartment: it was the paper that covered the cork, and in his impatience, Alejandro ripped it with the corkscrew.

Finally, he left, and Clara managed to cut out a wide variety of stars, all of them different and airy, as though they were made of lace. She spread them out on the floor, and even Asmodeus felt happy, purring for a short while. She would have liked to paste all those stars on the ceiling to greet Alejandro when he arrived, but she wanted to save the surprise for Christmas Eve.

Only Don Anselmo knew about her project because she was so enthusiastic that she had to tell someone. And Don Anselmo could help her; in addition to lending her the scissors, he had agreed to collect discarded packs of cigarettes from the street when he came home late at night and nobody would see him. Clara glued the silver paper to a piece of cardboard and cut out paper dolls, although making stars was far more fascinating because you had to fold the circles into six parts and cut them out in random patterns, and they always turned out surprisingly different.

There were only two days left till Christmas Eve when Clara told herself that she had enough stars to decorate an entire tree. There were twenty-three altogether: twenty-three stars that represented as many bottles of wine in ten days. It hadn't taken her long to discover where Alejandro's money went. Her throat knotted up with rage, and she felt like crying. She, who never touched a drop of wine, hardly. Her tears began falling copiously, as she thought about all the Roman candles she could have bought Chichón if not for those damn bottles of wine.

She cried for a good, long time, until she noticed a cruel gleam of happiness in Asmodeus's eyes. Asmodeus's eyes were identical to his master's; they caught the light in exactly them same way when his lips should have been smiling. Alejandro and Asmodeus smiled only with their eyes, ironically, mocking the world.

Clara recalled that afternoon when Alejando had taken the day off, and she had decided to do some housecleaning anyway. She had jostled a clay statue on the table with her feather duster. Alejandro shouted, "Be careful!" and jumped out of bed to catch it. He held it with both hands, lovingly.

"Do you really love your little statue?"

"It's not a little statue; it's an idol, for your information. And I don't love it one bit. I'm not attached to things."

"But you must like it a lot, anyway… Look how you're stroking it…"

"I'm stroking it?" he asked, astonished. And he tightened his fist with rage, breaking the idol's legs.

"You see?" he said, opening up his hand again so that Clara could witness the destruction.

"I'm not attached to things."

Clara stood there staring at him, fighting the tears that wanted desperately to escape from her eyes. Finally, swallowing hard, she managed to ask him:

"And Asmodeus? Don't you love Asmodeus, either?"

"So now the lady is jealous of the cat? Does she want me to break his legs, too? But don't think Asmodeus is the type who croaks just like that; that's why I like him. When I found him, he was just a couple of weeks old and he followed me down the street, howling his lungs out. I brought him home because I felt sorry for him, and I put him in a box to shut him up. I left it in a corner, next to a bowl of milk, and every morning I went to see if he had croaked. But he didn't, even though he was emaciated, so one day I took him outside to get some sun, and there you have him, perfectly healthy."

Clara looked at both of them, and at that moment, she confirmed they were laughing together, with their eyes.

He had brought her home with him out of pity, also, and had tossed her into a corner, but she was determined to take it just like Asmodeus, and the cat had no reason to laugh at her, not even now when she was crying for having lost her Roman candles.

"I'll do something about it, and sooner than they think. You'll see," she told the cat, threateningly. "No use in being so smug, you and your owner, and everybody else. If I need money, I know exactly how to get some for myself."

IX

*S*he put on the lavender dress that made her feel brave, and there were plenty of sailors, her specialty, in the neighborhood, but in spite of this conjunction of favorable conditions, she couldn't summon the courage to approach even one man. Two opposing forces struggled inside her, and she didn't know which side to take. On one side was the temptation of the Roman candles with the implicit possibility of decorating the Christmas tree, and her desire to put one over on Alejandro. On the other side, with the frozen smile she tried to direct at solitary passersby, was her firm conviction that she'd never put one over on Alejandro.

I'm not attached to things, he would tell her, so you can go straight to hell, and without getting out of bed or even changing position, he'd throw her out like a wretch, and she would have to start all over again, and she was so tired of starting over constantly, when in the long run, everything new turned out to be so much like everything old and familiar and despised. She sighed wearily, and a man passing by thought he understood that sigh and took her arm. Clara yanked herself away abruptly and desperately started running so she wouldn't have to begin the same old story once again.

She ran through the streets, turning corners without stopping, until she paused, out of breath, at the block where the tenement was. From the opposite end of the brightly-lit street, a familiar shadow was approaching.

"Don Anselmo!" Clara cried when she recognized him. He was her salvation.

"Clara, my child, what are you doing on the street at this time of night?"

"I don't know… I went out for a walk because I was bored."

"I understand, I understand. But this neighborhood is dangerous for a girl like you. Lots of nasty things could happen to you… Do you want me walk you home?"

"Walk me home? We're practically at the front door…"

"We could go for a little stroll…"

"Well, if you insist. But Don Anselmo, you know I can't get back too late."

"Of course, of course. We'll just walk right over there."

He put his arm around her waist, and Clara was ready to let him console her, but she thought about Alejandro again, and she suddenly grew rigid. He noticed.

"You seem upset, and it's very hot. How about a beer? There's a bar right over there, just four blocks away."

"Yes, it is very hot... Let's go, if you want."

They were only in the bar for half an hour, but Don Anselmo took full advantage of the time, playing up all his courtesy and chivalry to the maximum. He did it so skillfully that at last Clara dared asked him to lend her money to buy the Roman candles.

"Certainly, whatever you like," he replied, pulling out his billfold. "Of course, you're going to have to invite me to see your tree, okay? A special invitation..."

"Sure, if you want to come, the tree is for everyone. You'll also be able to see the Roman candles. They're so pretty. The kids wanted firecrackers, but I don't like them because they explode. But the Roman candles light up and fly like those shooting stars... If you want, you can make three wishes."

"And are you going to make three wishes? For my part, I'd be satisfied with just one..."

He looked into her eyes, and rubbed his leg against Clara's under the table, and since she didn't seem to notice, he felt encouraged enough to place his hand on her knee.

"Look, we're going to have a lovely party," he said, to distract her. "I'll see if I can get those firecrackers the kids wanted. It's against the law, and a policeman shouldn't do those things, but just this once... After all, Christmas doesn't come along every day. We're going to have a great time, more fun than we've ever had before, and these parties usually get pretty lively around midnight. But all those years before didn't count for me; only this year. It seems brighter now, because you're here. I'll help out with the little party, too, and I promise to get you the firecrackers. If you're afraid, come with me and I'll protect you..."

How nicely he speaks; it's lovely listening to him. But I mustn't encourage him. I'm going to stay with Alejandro during the party.

"It's getting late, Don Anselmo. "I'm going to have to go home now." She stood up.

"Oh! I forgot about your responsibilities. A pity these things exist. It was a pleasure chatting with you. I'll walk you back to the house, if it won't create any problems for you, of course."

Clara thought that Alejandro should be arriving any moment now, and she replied, "I'd rather go alone, you know. But please, watch me from over here. I really don't like walking around alone on these dark streets."

"As you wish, as you wish. And thanks for your company."

Clara held out her hand with an almost childlike seriousness and walked away happily because she had finally met a man who thought she was decent and who respected her. She had asked him to watch her as she returned home, not because she was afraid of the men she might meet on the way, but rather so that he wouldn't think she was what she really was.

Alejandro arrived home just fifteen minutes after her. He found her fast asleep.

The next morning, she asked Alejandro to take her to Parque Retiro to watch the Christmas preparations.

"What the hell preparations are you talking about? You can imagine that no one in Leandro Alem prepares for that idiotic holiday. I might be able to drum up more customers, but even that's not for certain."

"But I want to go and see you."

"See me? I don't have the slightest intention of playing the clown in front of you. I'm warning you, I won't give you the opportunity to laugh at me, so stop nagging. Not one more word on that subject. No one makes a fool of me."

"At least, Alejandro, at least could you bring your stuff home tonight and do the smoke trick just for me and tell my fortune? I get really excited when you do that!"

She tried to stroke his forehead, but he shrugged her off and turned around, and without replying he lay down in his favorite position, facing the wall.

Clara felt like crying, but she controlled herself because she knew quite well that he didn't like scenes, and any little thing could put him in a bad mood. Still, he had been so affectionate to her ten minutes earlier. She didn't understand him, but she didn't make any effort to understand him, either; she knew perfectly well that, despite what people say, men are much more complicated than women.

The only thing she could do was try to make the happy moments she had spent with him last a bit longer than they really did, to summon them up in her defense whenever she felt like crying.

That same afternoon, peering out the window, she saw the children bringing the tree, and she thought it wasn't worth the trouble of fighting with Alejandro about going to Parque Retiro if she had another possibility within her sights. She lay down at his side and said in a very gentle voice:

"Forgive me, I didn't mean to make you angry. I only wanted to keep you company, but if you don't like that, it's okay. I won't mention it again. Be nice, forgive me, and give me a little kiss…"

He had his back to her, tense and motionless, and he appeared not to have heard her, but out of the corner of her eye, Clara could see the points of the Roman candles peeking out of the old jug where she had hidden them that morning, and that gave her the energy to keep insisting. She insisted so long and so well, carefully caressing him as if she were afraid of offending him, that Alejandro finally surrendered.

"Okay, I forgive you, but don't bug me any more with that stuff about coming to see me. I'm fed up with that job; I'll have to do something else, something I really like."

As he slowly undressed her, Clara realized that her experience with men had had some purpose, after all.

Her sadness had evaporated, but it returned when he told her, just before leaving, "I'll be home later than usual tonight; I have some very important business to attend to with Marcovecchio, my partner."

He was already halfway down the stairs when he added: "I forgot to tell you I'm not working tomorrow."

From the landing where she had gone to see him off, Clara shouted with joy, and as soon as she saw him disappear, she ran back to the apartment and got down on all fours in order to retrieve a box from beneath the bed. She opened it lovingly and once more examined the stars and paper dolls she had cut out. The moment for hanging them on the tree had finally arrived. She'd leave the Roman candles where they were; she knew perfectly well that if she gave them to Chichón ahead of time, he wouldn't be able to resist the temptation of lighting them.

She ran down the stairs, arriving excitedly at the patio, where the children greeted her without enthusiasm. She didn't worry about that, though; the tree was there. It felt like it belonged to her. Little by little, she removed all the treasures from the box, and the children watched her in astonishment, handing her the strings. At last only the largest star was left, to be placed on top of the tree. As it was one of those she had made, she had the honor of placing it there. A boy brought her a chair, and she climbed up without being urged.

"Will you look at the nerve of that one!" remarked a woman who was washing sheets in the laundry to her neighbor. "She probably wants to show off her legs, up there like that. Lucky our husbands are at work. But if I were you, I wouldn't let my kids hang around with her; she's a tramp, and she might fill their heads with disgusting ideas."

"But, Doña Herminda, the children need someone to help them set up the Chirstmas tree."

"That's your business; I'm not getting involved. But if they come down with a shameful disease, I'm not going to be the one to take care of them for you while you go to the market, like when your Pochito got the measles."

Clara's clear laughter filtered down to the laundry, and the two women fell silent. The children formed a large circle around Clara, admiring the tree. Clara was watching the children, but she could see the Christmas tree reflected in their dazzled expressions. She was proud of her work, of having managed to awe them to that extent, and she would have liked to stay there for a long time, savoring the happiness of the others, but it was already growing late, and the mothers began to call their children in to supper, and the enchantment was breaking up. Clara and Chichón were left alone in the middle of the patio.

"The tree turned out great, huh?" the boy exclaimed, unable to conceal his enthusiasm.

"You see how right I was to help you?"

"Yeah, but you didn't keep your promise. Where are the fire-crackers?"

"I did keep my promise! I have Roman candles, but I won't give them to you till tomorrow night."

"Tomorrow! Why not today, just to see 'em? You could give me one, to try. Just one little one, to make sure the powder isn't wet."

"No," Clara said decisively. "There are just a few of them, so we'll save them all for tomorrow, when the time comes."

"Just one, don't be mean."

But Clara knew how to be firm and not let herself be persuaded easily, and Chichón had to run off because his father was calling him and threatening to come after him with a leather belt if he disobeyed.

Clara remained there alone for quite a while admiring her tree before she resigned herself to going back upstairs.

The night was growing dark and gloomy, and no matter how much

Clara strained her eyes, she couldn't see the tree from the garret window. She waited patiently for the moon to appear, but after midnight, she couldn't wait any longer, and picking up Asmodeus in her arms, she went downstairs on tiptoe to show someone her accomplishment. When he got to the patio, Asmodeus unconcernedly escaped, running off to scrutinize some parrots in a cage that hung out of reach. Clara felt disappointed because the cat hadn't even stopped to look at the tree outlined in shadows.

She stood there examining each and every star until she heard steps behind her and was forced to turn around.

"Beautiful decorations," a voice said. "I'm sure you made them by yourself. Those snot-nosed little ingrates couldn't have done it."

A man's arm slipped around her waist.

"Oh! Don Anselmo!" Clara protested, moving aside to avoid him. "You gave me a real fright! Do you really like it?"

"Fantastic. Let's see if we can put a few little candles on it tomorrow, to make it shine more… Too bad I'm on night shift now, but as soon as I'm done, I'll come running back here. You'll wait for me, won't you? I'm going to bring you a little surprise for Christmas. What do you think about that? A reward for having decorated our patio so nicely."

There was a pause, and then he added: "But why don't you come to my room for something to drink? I've got some cold, brewed mate; we could chat for a while…"

He drew very close, put his arm around her waist again, and tried to kiss the back of her neck, but he only managed to rub his mustache against her. Furious, Clara realized that he didn't regard her as decent at all, as she had hoped. Certain attitudes, certain pasts, must show on people's faces. But she didn't want to display her anger, and she regained her composure, answering in a pleasant way:

"Now I have to go upstairs. I came down to show the Christmas tree to Asmodeus the cat, but it looks like he's not that interested."

Then she hurried upstairs even though she knew that Alejandro would be returning later than usual that night.

"Did you see the tree last night?" was the first thing she asked Alejandro the next morning when he woke up.

"What tree?"

"The Christmas tree, in the middle of the patio…"

"I didn't even notice there was anything in the patio. I have serious worries on my mind, and I'm not in the mood to go around looking at idiotic things."

Clara dragged the chair over to the window and looked out over a small overhang.

"Come here, come here, you can see it from here. If you could just see how it's shining now with the sun right on it. It looks all lit up. Come on, look!"

"You think I'm about to get up for that? If you want to throw yourself out a third story window, go right ahead, but it would be better if you got down from that chair. Did you bring back the wine from the grocery?"

"Yes, one bottle. Come see the tree; I decorated it myself."

"I knew you were stupid, but I didn't know just how stupid!"

Clara closed her eyes.

"Then you won't come and see it? I did it for you."

"For me? What the hell does your nonsense matter to me?"

Clara bit down hard on her lips to hold back her disappointment and carefully climbed down from the chair. "I'm going to the bathroom," she said. She ran out of the room.

She stayed in there a long time. When she felt calm overtake her again, she slid open the bolt and climbed the stairs hurriedly to the warm, indifferent shelter of Alejandro's back. He had gone back to sleep.

In the afternoon, she had to go downstairs again to the grocery because Alejandro wasn't working, and he was thirsty. Sadly, she bought two bottles of wine; she would have preferred a little cider, or something like that, but he had remarked that it was a drink for fairies. It was nearly seven by the time she went downstairs, and she had to be careful to avoid Don Anselmo.

When she returned to the room, she found it empty. She decided to take advantage of Alejandro's absence to get dressed and put on her makeup. The prospect of the party had restored her good mood, and she hummed to herself as she rummaged through the boxes on the shelf in search of the one that held her flowered dress, the one she had been wearing when she met Alejandro. She combed her hair carefully and tied on a gauzy kerchief as a headband. Deep down, Don Anselmo was like every other man: no sensitivity. She smiled to herself in the mirror. The problem with women is that they're too sensitive, and they cry all the time. You have to be strong. All dressed up like that, she was a real dish. There was no reason to worry, especially not on Christmas Eve.

Thinking about Christmas Eve made her remember the Roman candles; she'd have to act very quickly in order to give them to Chichón before Alejandro came back from the bathroom.

When he entered the room, he found her sitting on the bed just as if nothing had happened.

"You look pretty," he said and sat down beside her, not to embrace her as she had hoped, but instead to take a swig from the bottle of wine on the nightstand. Then he stretched out on the bed, fiddling for quite a while with the ends of the kerchief Clara wore in her hair.

"Why'd you get all dolled up?" he asked, finally.

"To go to the party, of course."

"To the party? What party?"

"A party they're having downstairs. We're all going to get together on the patio and have some fun. They even put out tables and chairs, didn't you see them? Everyone has to chip in a few pesos to pay for the pastry and cider…"

"Pastry and cider, pastry and cider," he intoned. "How lovely – a real good neighbor policy. Do I look like an idiot to you? You think I'm going to waste my time and money on those jerks? You can just take off that pretty dress of yours, because you won't be needing it in here." His tone had become aggressive.

"But, aren't we going downstairs, then?" Clara asked him, in the hope that he was joking.

"No, my precious. We're-not-go-ing. We'll have a much nicer time here all by our lonesome."

"But it's Christmas Eve, Alejandro. That's something really important. You've got to celebrate and have a good time. You don't understand…"

"I understand everything, ma'am. And it makes me want to puke, your Christmas. Hand me the bottle so I can settle my stomach a bit."

His eyes were opaque; he had drunk too much. He was about to become dangerous. She couldn't refuse him the bottle.

"But if fun is what you're looking for, precious (and I'm calling you precious because you really are: precious, precious, precious)… If you want some fun, we can have lots of it right here, without anyone's help. I'm starting to get in the mood."

"But I promised to go downstairs…"

He got angry.

"And who did you promise, if I might ask? That cop with the mustache, the one who goes around chasing your tail? Aren't you even ashamed of making promises to a cop? You make me sick. But just so you'll see I'm not vengeful, I'm going to do you the huge favor of making you break your promise. That's what you get for hobnobbing with filth! And pass me the other bottle. Those bastards at the grocery make them smaller all the time, just to piss a guy off. Christmas, hah! Pass me the cup, too. I don't like to drink alone. And don't look at me with those lovesick cow's eyes. Drink, drink. That's it – bottoms up. Don't leave one drop. Like that."

Three times he filled her cup, and three times he forced her to turn it over to make sure not one drop was left. At last the empty bottle rolled under the bed.

"Now we're really going to have fun," he said, and grabbing her by the shoulders, he pushed her down.

To have fun you need to go slowly, slowly. Alejandro let himself be rocked by a certain beneficent wooziness, as if he were sailing a swift sailboat on a sunny morning.

Suddenly, just outside to the door, they heard a soft whistle, like someone calling. Alejandro leaped up.

"It's that filthy cop calling you. You're a bitch, a bitch! Whore!"

The wine settled in Clara's head and she was able to get her bearings.

"I know I'm a whore; everyone knows it. You don't have to shout it out loud. Even the cop knows; that's how he got the idea of coming after me. Not because I did anything wrong with him. I never did anything with him, never. I wanted him to think I was decent…"

"Swear you didn't fuck him."

"I swear! You can squeeze all you want, but I swear I didn't… I didn't go to bed with him."

"You're a lying piece of shit."

He grew suddenly calm, as if he were mulling something over. Clara watched him expectantly, and finally he said:

"No one plays me for a fool. You know that? You're not going to make a fool of me so easily. If you feel like going around cheating on me, don't ever set foot in here again, understand? And now get over here, because I don't like unfinished business."

X

*T*he only portion of the party Clara was able to see were three of her Roman candles whizzing by the garret window. She didn't even hear the laughter or the singing; she let herself be rocked gently by her disillusionment, and she fell asleep gradually like someone entering a warm, dark river.

After a long dream, she awoke to the pleasant sensation of having lost her bitterness, and as soon as Alejandro opened his eyes, he announced he wanted to marry her.

He had thought it over all night long; he had weighed the pros and cons, and he realized that the only way to hold on to her was by catching her unaware. For that reason he had proposed to her, just like that, off-handedly. But he had thought about it all night long, despite the wine rumbling around in his empty stomach. After all, he needed someone to torture subtly; Clara was prime material, and he didn't want to lose her. Besides, she was good in bed and did everything he asked, and she didn't run off at the mouth like other women he had known. Once they were married, she'd be obliged to follow him; he could happily quit his job at the amusement park and go around the world in search of something suitable for a man of his worth.

"We're getting married, you hear?" he repeated so there would be no doubt about it.

Clara wasn't altogether awake; her eyelids were drooping.

"But I don't know if I want to get married," she objected.

"Of course you want to – what else could you be after?"

"After? I'm not after anything. Before, yes – I wanted to get married, but now... I don't know any more. At least give me a little time to think it over. You're not in any hurry, right?"

Now she's trying to play hard-to-get, Alejandro thought, and maybe she'll run away on me with that cop.

"I'll give you until noon, but be careful, because if you take too long, I'll be the one to change my mind."

Clara got up and dressed to go to the grocery, but instead of putting the change purse in her bag as she usually did, she carefully took her white purse. She wanted to consult the little red paper with her fortune on it, which she had kept there since that night when an unknown Alejandro had handed it to her. At the second floor landing, she took it out of her purse and began unfolding it to find out whether or not she should marry him. She told herself she was a coward: she had always dreamed of getting married, and now when someone had seriously proposed to her for the first time, she was backing off, scared. The first floor landing was sufficiently lit to allow her to read, but she crumpled the paper in her hand without deciphering a single word because she was too much of a coward to do that, either: rather than discovering anything in it that might embitter the rest of her life, she preferred to bear the weight of her own responsibilities, knowing as she did that what isn't written can't happen, anyway. They had repeated that maxim to her for ten years, back in her village, when she attended Catholic Action meetings, so it must be an irrevocable, indisputable truth. But she didn't exactly trust Alejandro. He had given her three different fortunes, just like that, and he probably didn't remember that she had chosen the red one. Maybe what he wanted was to change the predetermined order of things and keep them all for himself.

The front door was closed, and Clara crossed the hallway in darkness. When she least expected it, a man's silhouette crossed her path.

"Naughty girl! Why didn't you come to the party last night like we agreed? I had a special bottle waiting for you in my room, and some other goodies…"

The rage Clara had felt when he called from outside her door returned intact, and she clenched her teeth and puffed out her cheeks to keep from insulting him.

"Why didn't you answer my call?" he insisted familiarly, drawing closer to embrace her.

"You louse, you louse," Clara uttered to herself, "taking me for some tramp. Your lap dog…" and it disgusted her that he would take the liberty of fondling her just when she was about to make such a serious decision.

"You're very rude. Let me go!" she said, suppressing the insults in order to keep her distance.

"Why should I let you go, darling, when we're so nice and comfy right here?"

"What do you mean, nice and comfy! You're going to be nice and comfy when my fiancé comes downstairs and finds you."

"Your fiancé!" he hooted scornfully.

"My fiancé, that's right. We're getting married next week, if you really want to know."

She gave him a shove and opened the front door indignantly. How easy, how simple things turn out to be. We're getting married next week, if you really want to know. She had wanted to know, too, and now she knew. It wasn't her fault if that guy pushed her into marriage; now she couldn't turn back. The serious decision had been made. She breathed a sigh of relief. And as she waited her turn at Don Pepe's grocery, she wondered if she would have the right to wear a white dress and a tulle veil over her face when she entered the church. She'd probably have to forego those wholesome customs... It was a shame.

She ran up the stairs, bottles and all, and reached the third floor out of breath.

"Let's get married," she told Alejandro as soon as she saw him, so he wouldn't change his mind.

"All right, let's get married." And he made her sit down by his side.

"Are you happy?" he asked her after a while.

"I don't know... I'm still not really used to the idea. Although nothing much will change from what we've got already, right?"

"Who knows... we're going to move far away. I'm fed up with this tenement."

"Do you love me?"

"No, I don't love anyone, you know that. But I feel okay with you."

The next day, he went out earlier than usual and stopped by City Hall. To make an appointment, just like going to the doctor, he told himself, and he turned in his papers and Clara's. They made him pay for the certificate, and they directed him to get a prenuptial examination at any hospital.

He returned from Parque Retiro at one-thirty in the morning. Clara was still up, biting on a pencil point and making calculations.

"I can make the dress with three of four yards of taffeta," she told him. "And since the church here is small, we don't have to have a lot of flowers."

Alejandro was too tired to object, but the business about the church weighed more heavily than his desire to sleep.

"Not in your wildest dreams, madam, will I take you to the altar. If those are your conditions, you can go find yourself another husband. For my part, the civil ceremony is plenty good enough. Don't give me any of that priest business, or I won't get married at all."

January third dawned as oppressively hot as any other summer day. After lunch – bread, sardines, peaches – Clara put on her flowered dress, struggled to make Alejandro put on a tie, and they went to City Hall. The most complicated part was finding witnesses: Alejandro had no friends. They finally convinced Chichón's mother and Marcovecchio, the carnival barker. They arrived late; there were already a few couples ahead of them, with relatives and friends. They formed small groups, talking and laughing out loud. Clara looked at the brides enviously because they all wore chic hats, and surely in a few days they'd have a church wedding. Some of them even smiled shyly without looking at their fiancés, as if they were virgins. But for sure, none of them had as handsome a husband-to-be as she did, and that was enough.

When it was their turn, they went into an enormous, empty room, and when they emerged ten minutes later, they were already married. With signatures and all, and even a registry book. They went to a bar to celebrate, and Clara concentrated on studying the white registry book that Alejandro had left on a table, and which had spaces on it for the names of twelve children, and she didn't hear Marcovecchio saying that if Alejandro insisted, they could go try their luck elsewhere, but he, as a partner, really didn't like running from place to place like gypsies instead of staying put in Parque Retiro with a job that was nothing out of this world, true, but at least it was steady work... Those things didn't matter to Clara; the phrases that the man from City Hall had pronounced to them were spinning around in her head and ringing in her ears: the wife must be faithful to her husband and follow him wherever he goes, and she must obey him, et cetera, et cetera.

For the very first time, she had a duty that didn't consist of earning money; she felt disoriented and happy at the same time.

The Head

I

Clara filled the basin with the water that was left in the pitcher and for the third time washed her eyes, her hands, and her arms up to the elbow. Close the shutters, the hotel owner had recommended; otherwise the room will be filled with flies. Her eyes ached from working in the darkness for so long, and her palms were covered with sweat. From the hotel kitchen came the nauseating odor of the stew they had eaten for lunch; they were probably reheating it for supper. It was late already, and she had to meet Alejandro at the carnival. She picked up her sequined embroidery to wrap it up in a towel; the dragon on the left side sparkled in the darkness. The one on the right side was barely begun, and Clara thought she had made the eye wrong... if she'd made a mistake, she'd have to undo the whole thing and start over. That's how sequins are; if you want to remove one of them, you have to take out all the ones that are on the same length of thread. Just like some men: a girl tries to pull a little decency out of them, but as soon as she tugs, all their other good qualities end up in her hand, too. The ones who seem the most well-mannered and shy turn out to be the customers who put on the biggest airs. Ancient history, of course. Now the present brought only the smell of heat and dust. Everything she did, said, or thought immediately turned grimy and dusty; not even her complicated dragon embroidery distracted her.

Every afternoon, in every provincial town through which they passed, she had to go pick up Alejandro when he left work, for if she didn't, he would just stand there, propped up against the first bar counter he could find, clutching a bottle of gin and trying to remember things he had forgotten years before. Nevertheless, at siesta time, before leaving the hotel, he prepared his equipment conscientiously, and lovingly tucked the playing cards and colored scarves into their mysterious pockets or into the false-bottomed trunk or into the magician's hat. But at the end of each day, he seemed drained, like someone whose soul had been emptied out, and Clara had to pick him up in order to give him the strength to return to the hotel. Even so, he was a hit with the children, although the more he heard them laugh, the more glasses of gin he needed afterwards, at closing time. He hated children, and at the bar he dreamed of adults who were beyond such easy astonishment and who could be his acolytes in some secret society. He would think about Fulcanellli or Gurdieff, and then he would kick the counter furiously because he realized that this was no destiny for a man, either.

Clara. As she walked down the dusty streets, she dreamed of being able to share Alejandro's dreams whenever she saw his eyes fixed on something she couldn't discover herself. She had been trailing after him for two months now, and not a word about his intentions, his plans, or even his love for her. Always following behind him and colliding with his silence.

She had left the main street behind, and now she passed in front of the low, impenetrable houses, some with serious, inscrutable walls separating them from the open countryside of the pampa. The women had placed their straw chairs out on the path and sat knitting amid all the dust, waiting for a gust of wind that wouldn't come. Farther off, an old man spilled buckets of water on his portion of tamped-down earth, and the children seized the opportunity to smear themselves with mud. But Clara took no interest in any of those landwrecked lives, as if she hadn't lived it herself back in Tres Lomas. Although the dust in Tres Lomas was more like sand, and it brought her an occasional recollection of that oh-so-distant sea. Now Alejandro wanted to lock her inside a circle which had only room enough for him, and little by little he was plunging her into absolute isolation. I forbid you to come see me, he told her again and again; you make me nervous. And Clara, obediently, stayed at whichever seedy hotel it was, trying to keep busy with her embroidery without even daring to wish for anything too intensely. She went from town to town like a bouncing ball, without stopping to talk to anyone, looking only for the road from the hotel to the bar or to the café or to the general store where her husband would be submerging himself in his gin. There was only one hope she kept repeating to herself on each train journey, whenever she felt most oppressed and nauseated. I'm going to have a baby, she told herself, but a single glance at Alejandro was enough to make her realize that not even that could be true because everything that might possibly happen to her was controlled by the force of that will which didn't believe in love.

A car passed by, and instinctively she covered her face with a gauze handkerchief; eyes closed, she waited for the cloud of dust to settle. Before, at least, when Marcovecchio was with them, things had gone better, and it was he who had organized the schedule of carnivals and trips. At least he was cheerful and talkative; with him Clara could have met other people, those who really worked at the carnivals, the ones who got together at night to drink wine and sing plaintive songs accompanied by guitars. But the fight had been inevitable. Alejandro organized it masterfully, creating something intangible between the two men; he nourished it so that the tension would mount day by day, until his partner of many years couldn't stand it any more and exploded one day without really understanding why:

"I'm fed up with all this! I'm going back to the capital! You two can go on rotting in these lousy little hick towns if you want. Wasting away. As far as I'm concerned, you won't see hide nor hair of me any more. Or any other part of my anatomy, for your information."

Clara looked at him enviously. At least there was someone who was able to shout at Alejandro, able to return to the city. But Marcovecchio didn't see the gleam in her eyes, and slamming the door behind him, he went away forever. Only then did Alejandro manage a smile.

Rotting. That was the word. Wasting away. Nothing remains of you as a person in these towns; everything disappears little by little, gets erased under a white layer of dust. Locked in a coffin, locked in the middle of the unfathomable, alien countryside. At least in my village every roof, every little tree in the plaza, every fencepost was my friend. Now I'm a stranger to everyone – the magician's wife, a tramp. Almost a foreigner, badly regarded by carnival employees and outsiders alike.

Marcovecchio had gone away without even turning around to look at her, to feel a little bit sorry for her. She picked up her embroidery and sat down to work; at that point, the first dragon displayed only his golden crest, and the sequins sparkled in her hand. But Alejandro's smile lasted just for a moment, extinguishing itself immediately. Big drops of perspiration ran down his forehead; now that we're free, we can go to the sea, she had told him to perk him up, but her words only triggered an explosion of all his repressed anger and made his triumph seem bitter.

She felt the heat weighing on the back of her neck. The sun pursued her down the street. A group of young girls, barely younger than she, had gathered in the doorway of a bakery to eat ice cream and remark on people passing by. Although she would have liked to have an ice cream, too, she decided not to breach that wall of womanhood. Nonetheless, her real place was there, as it had once been before, laughing and eating ice cream on a hot Sunday afternoon.

The carnival was already shut down when she arrived; she went directly to the general store a couple of steps away. As she had anticipated, Alejandro had his elbows on the tin counter, staring blindly at the black piles of espadrilles on the display shelf.

The owner of this new hotel was friendly. He had given her permission to remain in the dining hall at siesta time because there wasn't enough light in her room to embroider. She had only a small window, practically at ceiling level, and a door that faced the back patio where the toilets were, and where the garbage cans and empty bottles piled up.

That same morning Clara had bought the package of green sequins and begun the second dragon's tail. Her eyes hurt. She decided to rest a bit and count the people passing by. The dining room window was closed, and the shallow design of flowers in the insecticide powder on the glass invited her to lay her open hand down, leaving the imprint of her palm. She liked those subtle, symmetrical flowers; she had watched the owner carefully making them with a rolling pin. She tried to contain her breath, to repress her sighs so they wouldn't fly away in a thousand specks of dust. If she erased the flowers, they would throw her out of the dining room, and she wouldn't be able to count the people going by as she waited for Alejandro. But no one passed by. In those town, *siesta* hour is always desolate and deserted. And the farther inland they went, the longer people took to poke their noses outside their houses after noon.

Alejandro had the gift of making things change in subtle ways. Clara realized that they had never been in such a wretched hotel before, and to top it all off, they had been obliged to take the worst room. And that wasn't all: the carnival had changed, too.

Alejandro was unable to remain with the same people for very long, and now he had to be content with setting up his old tent and doing his tricks at a fair, surrounded by street vendors and the occasional fortune teller. If only Marcovecchio hadn't left them...

However, Alejandro knew an extraordinary number of juggling tricks; she had spied on him one night as he rehearsed a new move: she half closed her eyes, pretending she wasn't watching, and a shimmering sensuality ran up her spine. She saw scarves – purple, yellow, orange – that appeared and disappeared, almost brushing her face. If only she could find out where he hid those scarves, one night she might be able to get up silently and wind them around her naked body and dance and spin and remember when she had all the men in the world entirely to herself.

The scarves flew, knotted together, and came untied again. Their touch must have been like a very young girl's, shy and caressing, warm and fleeting, asking for much more than it could give. But Alejandro made the scarves and caresses disappear for good, as he stood alone in the middle of the room, very much in charge of himself, and of Clara's emotions.

A small boy dragged a box on tiny wheels along the burning street. Clara wanted to call him and ask him if he was going to see the magician at the fair, ask him to find out where the magician hid his colored scarves after the show, but she stopped herself in time and kept on embroidering the dragon with the furled tail.

She couldn't find any more sequins in that town where everything was gray. Poor Asmodeus. He could have kept her company despite his mistrust, like when they lived in the tenement. But Asmodeus was lost forever. She had been there when Alejandro put him in the bag together with the cobblestone. The last thing he did before leaving the city was to throw him into the Riachuelo, without remorse, because he couldn't take him along. He's mine; I can do anything I want to him, he had said, more to himself than to Clara, to whom he owed nothing, not even an explanation.

"Listen, lady. You're going to have to hurry a little. The boss ordered me to sweep the floor."

He was a fat boy wearing a grease-stained undershirt. He had to be another landwrecked casualty from the city; country people don't smell of sweat like that. Clara wrinkled her nose in disgust but, as the boy was her only opportunity to talk to someone, she made the best of it and replied pleasantly:

"Of course. I'm leaving right away. I don't want to get in your way. Just one second while I tie a knot, and that's that."

"Hey, look at that! What a pretty design you're making there! Can I see?"

"Of course…"

"So many colors… But what a weird animal! Did you make it up?"

"No one made it up. It's a dragon."

"It's got to be ferocious, huh?"

"Not at all. The one that's finished already is called Asmodeus."

"Asmodeus? Why Asmodeus? That's a devil's name."

"No, it's the name of a cat we had who's dead now."

"But that one you've got there won't die on you, that's for sure!" and he belched out a garlic-tainted laugh.

"What's for dinner tonight?" Clara asked.

"Beef broth and meat *empanadas.*"

"Yum! I hope Alejandro will be in a good mood..."

It was too much to ask. Alejandro was not in a good mood. He pushed his dish of *empanadas* aside furiously, saying that they were made from leftovers, and made such a repugnant face that he ended up taking Clara's appetite away. He didn't even try a mouthful of the cheese and jellied fruit dessert, in spite of the fact that they couldn't possibly have been made of leftovers.

"What's the matter?" Clara asked him, bitterly.

"Nothing, nothing at all. What do you think is the matter?"

The other people in the dining room eventually turned around to see why he was shouting. Embarrassed, Clara attempted to calm him down.

"I was just trying to help you..."

She, who had lived so well before, and who now had to drag herself on the ground like that because one day in January she had sworn to be faithful to a husband... It was too much. Alejandro was too selfish; he ought to let her earn a few pesos, lend her to others a bit, and stop shouting as though everything that happened to him were her fault.

"If you'd just let me work to help you out..." she insisted.

Naturally, she couldn't find any respectable customers in a miserable little hellhole like this. She'd have to go back to Buenos Aires, where there was no dust or heat, because you could go out at night. She felt capable of facing anything. With new shoes and a nice perm, she might even dare stroll along Florida Street in search of wealthy patrons. But better than anything, even better than Florida Street or Santa Fe Avenue, would be to go to Mar del Plata. At the seashore, not only could she find very rich customers, but also waves, foam, sand. She felt her body expanding with anticipated happiness.

"If I had a job, we could even go to the seashore..." she ventured to confess to Alejandro.

"So you want to work, huh? You really think you could hold down a real job?... All right, if you want work, I'll find you work. But afterward don't go around complaining it's too much for you."

Nothing could be too much. Nothing worse than these hotels, this desolation. The only thing here was her hatred of this life, a hatred as squat and round as a coin; she felt it growing inside her, stretching and wiggling as if it were a child.

She tried to smile at Alejandro, but it was too late. He had already started believing that Clara was escaping through his fingers. She was flighty; she'd slip away without his being able to hold her back. In order to dominate her, to absorb her completely, it wasn't enough to leave her alone in a hotel room, abandoned. Clara would always find an escape so she could think about something else, so she wouldn't be trampled by him. And he had to take control of her somehow; that's why he had married her, to dominate her, to have her at his feet. He would have to humiliate her, perhaps, so she'd bend in two and surrender to him. So a single glance from him would shrink her at his whim.

Clara smiled at him again. Openly, this time. She was escaping from him – what the hell! She was slippery, amorphous. But he kept her close at hand, and when she least expected it, he'd trap her. He had to humiliate her – why hadn't he thought of it before?

"I know a job that would be good for you. You don't have to know anything to do it. It's a job where you don't do anything, perfect for someone useless like you. Today a guy told me about a fair that's passing through that needs an Aztec Flower, a head without a body. You'd be just right for it. But later on don't tell me you don't like it. If we accept, we're committed. All right? Fine, tomorrow I'll buy the material to build the set."

II

*C*lara felt happy. It was something inexplicable and almost forgotten, a feeling to which she was unaccustomed. Happiness bubbled up in her, spilling outside the limits of her body; she was surrounded by an aura of happiness that made her leap and dance and wouldn't leave her alone. "Pass me the hammer," Alejandro would say, and Clara hummed, "hammer, hammer," circling around the hammer without being able to find it. "Come here, help me hold this board," Alejandro would tell her, and she ran over to hold the board, wrinkling her brow because she wanted to do her job conscientiously. The heat, the flies, the dim light in the room – they didn't bother her any more. Shoulder to shoulder with Alejandro at last, helping him build something. She had never before felt so close to him except in bed, but bed didn't count, because that was a different sort of thing, a horse of different color. That's the way marriage should be: two people making an effort to build something together.

He seemed content, as well, muttering under his breath: the box is turning out like a dream, a dream, sweet dreams… Now, I just have to paint it before I install the mirrors and… *voilà!*

Such pretty mirrors, and all for me. Eight shiny mirrors, and so nicely cut. Eight big mirrors to cover me up, just for me. We'll have a booth in a real amusement park, the kind that travels like a circus all around the world, thanks to me. We'll hang around with jolly people, people who laugh, at last. And nobody will be able to make me stay away from the fair, because I'll *be* the fair. And going from city to city, one day we'll reach the sea…

"The sea, the sea, the ocean waves," she hummed.

"What are you talking about?"

"Nothing, nothing, I was just singing."

"I heard something about slaves, I don't know…"

"Not slaves, waves. With a *w*. Do you think some day we can go to the sea?"

"Leave me alone with your sea! When you get something into your head, not even God Almighty can get it out. One more time, madam, I repeat that you can't go to the Atlantic coast in summer because the beaches are filled with fat cats who wouldn't even dream of coming to see us. We're only good for poor hayseeds who've never seen anything worthwhile in their lives."

"That's what *you* say, but my act could be sensational. The wonder of the century. Something people will trample one another and pay a fortune to see."

"Sensational, is it? There are, have been, and will be millions and millions of Aztec Flowers in this world, and they all do the same thing as you without anybody blinking an eye. Millions and millions of idiotic lopped-off heads, and not one that's out of the ordinary."

"Maybe I can…"

"Maybe you can. Do it without tricks: I'll cut your head off, and you'll work it out so you can flirt and smile, like that, all charming. And I'll hold your head in the palm of my hand and we'll become millionaires."

"You're disgusting. You want to cut my head off and then you expect me to act lively."

"Bah! You couldn't even try to do anything out of the ordinary."

He shrugged his shoulders. Fucking life – didn't give him a chance. Still, it would be fun to try. He'd have to look into some alchemy formulas.

She wouldn't let herself become disheartened so easily. She began to sing a song she had made up, something like: Hooray! Hooray! Today's my day! /I've got no body, I'm just a head./I close my eyes, but I'm not dead. /I've got a mouth, and I can smile./And God is with me all the while.

"Don't yell like that! Stop making a ruckus! And quit jumping around. You're making me nervous. You're not fifteen any more, acting like you're not right in the head."

"I'm right in the head, my dear sir. You're mistaken. I'm right in the head. I *am* the head! Aren't I the head without a body?"

Alejandro scratched the nape of his neck indifferently.

"Okay, we've done enough for today. It's getting dark; we'll finish tomorrow."

"Tomorrow? Don't be mean. Let's finish it today so I can rehearse."

"As though you had anything to rehearse. Even the most dimwitted tramp can be an Aztec Flower. We'll finish it tomorrow because I don't have to go to work. Let's do it calmly. The artistic work is my part, since I have to construct the box. The rest of it is a cinch. Now I'll measure your neck for the opening…"

He put his hands around her neck as if to strangle her, pushed her gently towards the bed and threw himself on top of her.

Clara felt achingly happy. Alejandro had never been that way before, never. From that moment on, they'd do everything together; now they were united and everything was starting over. Let's forget about the past, Alejandro.

After making love, Alejandro reached out to the nightstand and took his pack of cigarettes. He lit one but forgot to smoke it, and it burned down between his fingers. He was bewildered: he had managed to conquer Clara through happiness, not by shame or humiliation as he had thought. The evidence made him feel bad, almost. Clara, so mysterious, who concealed impenetrable ideas behind her childish words. Clara, who never talked about herself, let herself be won over by a small, simple, even useless pleasure. His mission would be to make her happy always, so not even one particle of her remained beyond his reach and his understanding. But he felt worn out ahead of time. Tough work, this business of making people happy. Tough, and without compensation. It wasn't the same as making her suffer; making someone suffer gives you a nice little warm feeling in your stomach while the other person groans and squirms.

He squashed out the cigarette against the nightstand and lit another. Cigarettes and people are made to be squashed; it's much better than smoking them or using them. There are some people who don't squash their cigarettes, who throw the butts away carelessly, just like that. They're people without passion. On the other hand, certain others, those who get angry at the poor butt in the ashtray and shred it as if it were a flower, those are the ones you should love, or hate, and above all, fear. Alejandro squashed his cigarette butts with fury. Then he abandoned them.

Clara didn't smoke: that way, she could avoid useless daydreaming and concentrate fully on her new-found happiness. She spent a sleepless night, but she realized that finally she was to fulfill her destiny, the red fortune, the passionate one, the one she herself had chosen: she needed to erase everything she had done until then, the horrible and not-so-horrible things, and throw them into the trash. She stirred in bed, unable to contain her excitement. She made the elastic creak.

To stop thinking about that past which ruined her present, and to look forward. They would work together, she and Alejandro, each one announcing and giving his all to the other's act. One day they'd be hired as a live act for a movie house. And later in a theater, with real velvet curtains and an orchestra. She recalled the dining room in the hotel back in Tres Lomas, which had been a theater once, and which still had its very high ceiling, and its darkness, and those long, long curtains that had been red but had turned brown, and which you had to pass through to get to the counter. Ever since she was a girl, every time she entered that dining room, she would dream of being a variety show star. She had done well by marrying Alejandro, after all. She felt like waking him and talking to him about her plans. Together they'd make plans for the future. She couldn't stop moving around, and the elastic creaked more furiously each time. She leaned her head against his back, smooth and warm, and hugged it tightly as though it were a nest. Alejandro grumbled and without turning over, he asked: "Do you feel sick, or what?"

"I feel very good," and she added a new element to the construction of her happiness: he had asked her if she felt sick; he was worried about her health. No one had ever asked her if she felt sick, ever, except maybe Don Mario, who was quite paternal. Of course, there was no question of turning back; just concentrate on the present.

She would have liked to get up at dawn to finish her mirrored box, but Alejandro was still sleeping, and she didn't want to wake him. You've got to be careful with happiness; it's such a fragile, precious thing. It might break if you even look at it too closely.

Alejandro awakened at ten-thirty, and Clara made him a cup of coffee on the Primus stove that went with them everywhere.

"Are you going to paint it?" she asked him, pointing to the frame he had constructed the day before.

"Yes. We'll finish it this afternoon."

"And what color are you going to paint it? I'd like it to be red, but it could also be green, or yellow."

"You can't control your disposition, can you? You get carried away by your fantasies. Can't you see this contraption is supposed to be a table?

Ergo: it has to be brown, and only brown. You'll see – when the mirrors are put in, the illusion will be perfect. A table with four fine legs and nothing in between them."

"And my head will rest on top of the table?"

"Of course."

"How wonderful! I'll smile at everyone, and wink my eye, and even stick out my tongue at them if I feel like it; a head without a body doesn't know what it's doing."

"Yeah, go on, be a smartass, and you'll see what happens to you. Now hurry up and hand me the paint can that's under the bed. At noon I've got to go see the boss of that traveling circus. After all, we're still not really sure they'll accept us."

"Aren't you going to have lunch with me?"

"No. I'll have lunch with him, but it's for your own good. They don't have an Aztec Flower. I'm almost sure they'll give you a contract, and me, too, I hope."

"It'll be fantastic!" Clara shouted, throwing her arms around his neck and staining her dress with paint.

Alejandro returned at three in the afternoon. When Clara heard his footsteps in the hall, she leaped out of bed and opened the door in her slip.

"What did they tell you?"

"Don't shout, don't shout. People are sleeping."

"Since when have you been so considerate! Didn't they give us the contract?" She shook him to make him reply once and for all.

"They already have two magicians; they don't want to have anything to do with me. I'm only good for announcing your act."

"What does that matter? This way, we'll be able to work together... I've almost finished the dragons on your jacket. You can put it on when you announce me; too bad I'll have to sew up the secret pockets. They won't do you any good any more. Although you could always do a little sleight-of-hand to distract the people watching me, so they won't catch on to the trick."

"Turning tricks... that's your specialty."

Clara paid no attention to him. "Besides, you can announce me with a lot of bla-bla-bla, like Marcovecchio did. Remember how nice he talked? He was a genius at announcing you, huh? Are we going to work in a theater or a circus? How pretty a circus must be on the inside, with wild animals and horses and clever monkeys. All clever ones. I went to the circus four times. And you?"

"Piss off with your circus and your monkeys! It's just another carnival like all of them, each one in his own booth and manage as best you can. You've even got to attract your own customers..."

"You're better than anyone else at that. You'll get millions of customers, and I'll be the queen of the carnival. A queen without a body, but a queen, anyway. Do you think I could wear a little crown?"

"What I think is that you should shut up. You can also go get me a bottle of beer. I'm dying of thirst."

Clara put on her dress and slippers and went to the dining room in search of some hotel employee. She didn't dare call out or bang on the counter with her hands, so she had to wait a long time. When she returned with the beer, she discovered that Alejandro had fallen asleep crossways on the bed, naked.

She sat down on the remaining free corner and began admiring his body: he was as lithe as a sleeping tiger. She watched him for a long time; then she got bored and began to examine her box, which was already beginning to take shape. The only thing left to do was add the mirrors, which were leaning against the wall, reflecting her feet hanging a few inches above the floor. They're going to cover me up completely. What a shame – I don't exactly have a bad figure… but no, it's not a shame at all; it's a blessing from heaven because at last I'll be able to work with my head, all alone, without this body that's gotten in my way and caused me problems. As my teacher used to say, you've got to use your head… and yet, I wasn't a bad student, not at all, but there must've been something missing… Now I'm going to be able to use my head and nothing more than my head. I've got no reason to complain.

She kneeled down in front of the mirror and began to smile.

When Alejandro woke up, the first thing he said was: "Why didn't you wake me right away? Don't you realize it's very late and we have to finish this gadget tonight?"

And then he added, "Ugh! This beer tastes like puke! It's boiling hot…"

He put on his underwear and touched the paint on the contraption to see if it was dry.

"How is it ever going to dry in this humidity?"

You're griping too much; you'll spoil all my happiness. You've gotten used to complaining. Now you can't stop. To change the subject, she said aloud: "When do we start working?"

"We'll start, we'll start! As if I haven't been working all my life…"

"But I haven't… And I want to start so we can always be together and never be apart."

She kissed Alejandro on the back of his neck.

"Ugh, stop bothering me. You're tickling me," but he laughed.

She realized she could continue, and she kissed him, this time on the cheek.

"You're worse than a mosquito."

"But I'm a mosquito that loves you a lot…"

Alejandro grabbed her passionately and planted a big, wet kiss on her mouth.

"That one was no mosquito," she said. "It was a big, hippopotamus kiss."

Everything turns out to be so easy when you're happy. A few kisses, and she had already calmed Alejandro down. Maybe it was her fault that he had been so harsh and heartless before; what he needed was a little tenderness.

Alejandro placed his hands around her neck.

"Do you have a tape measure? We're going to measure so I can saw a whole in the cover."

She handed him the tape measure, and he wrapped it around her neck. Then he exclaimed, whistling with admiration: "Less than twelve inches! Nice little neck for strangling. I could do it with one hand."

"Just try. If you think I won't defend myself… I'll bite you, I'll scratch you, and I'll kick and everything."

"We'll see about that tonight. Now pass me the saw and hold the lid for me. We can't waste time; at dawn we're leaving for Entre Ríos."

"Already? In circus wagons and all that?"

"No, no. By train, like nice, happy, middle class people. We'll take one or two cars, and they'll pay for everyone's trip."

"And is the trip long?"

"I have no idea… We have to change trains in the capital. Entre Ríos is far away. We're going to Urdinarraín, a city."

"A city! Much more important than all these stinking little towns. We're making progress. Oh, Alejandro, be careful with that saw!"

Alejandro carefully sawed a semicircle in each lid and screwed the hinges against the edges of the table. The lids opened upwards, and in the middle was an opening as if they were stocks.

Clara was beside herself with awe. Her husband was the cleverest in the world, able to construct the most magical, unexpected things.

"You're a genius – you do everything so well."

"I'm an architect who's only good for household projects…"

Clara wondered why he became so sad when all she did was praise him.

"Let's put in the mirrors," she said, to ease his sadness. "Will my head be reflected in all of them?"

"Your head, thank God, won't be reflected in any of them. But go ahead and stick it in, because at three a.m. we have to be at the station."

He took one of the mirrors, placing it against a board that crossed the table legs diagonally.

"Do you have to put it that way, on the inside? Then I'm not going to fit..."

'Hey, you'll have to make yourself smaller. And don't give me such a hard time because now the delicate work begins. Pass me another mirror, quick, or this one here will slip out of place on me."

"Imbecile!"

The cry remained floating in the air, and Clara didn't dare lift her gaze; she could only look at her hands, surprised, as if they didn't belong to the rest of her body. At her feet shone the pieces of broken mirror. She couldn't remember the crash or the lights shooting off the gleaming mirror one moment before, as it fell. She saw only her opaque, sweaty, treacherous, slippery hands. It had slipped through them effortlessly, without so much as a warning, with a certain grace. Clara started to cry; her entire body shook with sobs as Alejandro looked at her with half-closed, accusing eyes.

Imbecile, imbecile, imbecile, she repeated to herself with each spasm, and Alejandro insulted her, too, without needing to say a single word.

He opened his mouth after a long silence: "You, you had to go and ruin everything. You go around bringing bad luck. For seven years, in case you want to know. If we can't find a glazier in Urdinarraín t cut us a mirror like the one you just dropped, we might as well hang ourselves from the same tree."

Enraged, he removed the boards from the table, wrapped everything carefully in an old blanket, and tied up the package with cord. Clara blew her nose loudly before asking him, "Aren't we going to try out the table?"

As usual, he didn't bother to reply.

III

*T*he train trip didn't differ much from those Clara had taken before, crossing the Pampa with Alejandro. True, the other passengers were lively, laughing and passing the bottle, some of them singing. They were all going to be colleagues, but she couldn't speak to them because out of the corner of her eye, she watched Alejandro, sullen and furious, self-absorbed, with his arms folded over his chest. In the opposite seat sat a fat woman who opened her wicker picnic basket every so often to pull out something to eat. As she chewed, her cheeks distended, and Clara couldn't stop staring at her, impressed. At last the fat woman realized she was being watched, and she offered Clara a sandwich on white bread from a stack she had just extracted from the basket. No thank you, Clara replied in a tiny voice so that Alejandro wouldn't hear her.

"Go on," the other woman insisted, "try them. They're nice and fresh. I always wrap them in a damp napkin so they won't dry out."

"No, thanks, I'm not hungry," even though she was dying of hunger because she hadn't had a bite since lunchtime the day before. "At least this way you'll pay for the mirror," Alejandro had told her, and since she really did want to pay for the mirror, she refused what she was offered, in an act of contrition.

The fat woman forgot about Clara and meticulously began dispatching her pile of sandwiches.

In the morning fog, Clara stared at interminably flat landscape, interrupted occasionally by a handful of trees. The cows and the wheat were peaceful and indifferent; only the wild horses ran with their manes blowing in the wind. Tres Lomas couldn't be too far from here, but years ago she had cut all ties with her home town, and she couldn't lean on that hope. Alejandro had fallen asleep, and Clara knew that even in his dreams he was sorry he had married her. He wasn't the only one; she, too, sometimes regretted having taken such a serious step without even giving it a thought, as if it were a game.

The fat woman addressed her again, and she was startled.

"What did you say?"

"I asked if you wouldn't happen to have a newspaper that you don't need. We're going to have to close the windows and seal everything up because the dust is getting hellish. It even gets in between your teeth."

Clara replied no, she didn't have a newspaper, and she was astonished to see that the tall row of sandwiches had already disappeared. To conceal her surprise, she ran her fingers through her hair, pretending to adjust a rogue curl: she noticed that her hair was hard and dry. If only she could go to some beauty parlor so she'd have a hairdo worthy of her début... But Alejandro won't even give me five pesos. I'm going to have to wash it myself and roll it up in strips of paper as soon as I get to the hotel.

"Who can give me a newspaper?" the fat woman shouted without warning. "I'm going to have to close the window on account of this damn wind!"

"Stick your ass out the window; then there won't be even a crack left open!" someone replied from the back of the wagon, and everyone laughed. Everyone except the fat woman, naturally, and Clara, who wasn't in the mood for jokes.

Finally the fat woman found a newspaper, went to the toilet which was between two of the cars, returned with the paper quite wet, and carefully placed it around the edges of the window to seal up all the spaces. That task took her a long time, and when she was done, she collapsed onto the hard wooden seat with a sigh of relief.

"Now we'll be better off, you'll see," adding, trying to make conversation with that poor girl who looked so serious and sad, "You're new here, aren't you? You'll see that we're all good folks, and when the tents are up, we all get along real well... I've got a ball-toss booth, you know? I make a pyramid out of cans, and the people throw cloth balls at them. There are some nice prizes. It's lots of fun. We always get a lot of young people, which I like. Before, I had shotguns, but they give me the creeps. I prefer balls. And you, what do you do?"

"Me? I'm the Aztec Flower."

"The Aztec Flower? We haven't had one around here for a long time. The last one left one year and three months ago, to be precise. One fine day, she said she was fed up with spending her life locked in a box and she stayed in Bragado with a plumber... My name's Chola, Chola Pedrazzi. What's yours?"

Clara was so happy to have someone speak to her that she concentrated on listening intently and wasn't prepared to respond. Finally she managed to pronounce: ""Clara Hernández...""

"Have you been an Aztec Flower very long?"

"No, I'm just starting. Before, I did other things, but this is the first time I have to use my head in my work. I'm very happy..."

"Well, you sure don't look it."

The porter came along with his basket of drinks, and Chola Pedrazzi bought a beer from him. Nothing for me, Clara had to tell him. Nonetheless, her throat was so parched, she felt that it would split open at any moment. Alejandro kept on sleeping with his head resting against the partition of the car. Better that way – he couldn't look at her with those accusing eyes.

After long, numbing hours of travel, they reached Once, a station that Clara would have preferred to forget. They had to go to Lacroze to catch the train to Entre Ríos. The tents and other general supplies had gone on a truck with the boss. Alejandro found out what time the second train was to leave, and as there was time, he decided to take the bus.

They crossed the plaza. Clara recalled that other green plaza with its tower in the grassy square, its waiting post. I want to break free of Alejandro, run away. Go back there to the side entrance of Parque Retiro where I can mull over my memories and maybe catch a glimpse of that little bit of happiness I had once and find Victor or Toño o any one of those guys again who always stayed the same and didn't change their moods like they'd change their shirts. I'd like to escape, but the heat's gotten to me and my heels are digging into the melted asphalt; things that I don't want always hold me back or push me forward like... what do you call it?... a puppet without a string.

Meekly, but filled with rage, she went to the end of the line for that damned bus that would take her to the other station, to keep on going, surrounded by the rattling of trains and Alejandro's vindictive silence.

This is the destiny you chose, after all. Don't be chicken.

They got off the bus at Lacroze Station. Alejandro told her, "Wait for me here." He gave her a handful of one-peso bills and disappeared behind the revolving door of the café where a long table had already been set up for the people from the carnival. Clara, who remained at the kiosk in the station so she wouldn't get too far away, allowed herself to buy just a cheese sandwich and an orange drink to fool her stomach and all the other internal organs that were clamoring inside her. She didn't leave a tip for the kiosk vendor, and she wrapped up the change carefully in her handkerchief: she had to contribute something to pay for the broken mirror.

On the train to Entre Ríos, Alejandro naturally chose the last seat in the car, where nobody could watch them and where there was no fat lady to bother Clara. Fatigue overcame her during the trip, and she fell asleep without really understand what had happened. When she awoke, the train was floating miraculously on the Paraná River, and Clara couldn't resist getting out of the car to explore the ferry and climb up to the bridge, where a compact group of passengers was squeezed together. Below, the river passed by slow and thick, making you want to close your eyes. Clara would rather have been sitting on the floor like that group of girls with their legs dangling over, and hanging on to the rail, but there are many things a woman alone cannot let herself do. Loneliness is like that: it's no so much the lack of company that's bothersome as the impossibility of doing a thousand little things you feel like doing, but which can only be done in a group: rocking on the swings in the park at night, watching a billiards game, sitting with your legs hanging over an abyss. Maybe even more than running after men so much, she would rather have found herself a few girlfriends, the kind you can laugh with. She stood there with her elbows resting on the rail, unthinking, trying to imagine that the green color of the islands was caressing her face. I'd be happy there, without dust or heat or trains, all day long with my feet in the water and my head beneath the trees.

A boy was asking his father questions: Are there a lot of islands in the river? Are there many animals on the islands? Do the snakes bite hard? And the father always replied "Mo' o' less" to every question, without even a change in intonation. Clara imagined that the people from Entre Ríos must be as sweet as their accent, with that drawl stretching out lazy as the river. She walked away, thinking that crossing the river was almost like seeing the sea. Almost.

The crossing took two hours, and when they made her get back on the train, she sat down next to Alejandro, saying, "My head aches."

"Nice job; that's what you get from staying out in that brutal sun, so stop complaining."

He knew, however, that he had no right to treat her that way, she who had spent an entire day without eating, nearly without sleeping, and not one complaint out of her. Deep down, he really admired her… He wanted to control her, and yet he admired her: it was annoying. That trusting head resting on his shoulder made him nervous. She was good: he condemned her to a dog's life, but instead of asking forgiveness, he burdened her with reproaches. How unfair, but he couldn't help it. Others had to pay for what he should have been but wasn't. His need for revenge was insatiable and relentless and made no exceptions for anyone. Least of all for Clara, with all her valor and her generosity, a whore he had picked up on the streets. He hated her. He hated her, and he had married her. Precisely for that reason, for that very reason, he hated her.

Clara couldn't manage to fall asleep on Alejandro's shoulder. An intense current flowing from that other body shook her, wouldn't give her any peace, stole all the good that could come from without because it managed to agitate the waters within her. Alejandro's hatred was powerful; it polluted her. I hate him, she told herself. I hate him. And afterwards: It's impossible; I've gotten sunstroke. I'm trembling because I have fever. I hate him. And she shut her eyes tight so she could see the colored lights that transformed themselves into enormous suns, blinding her.

Alejandro felt as if he had captured the truth, and he was astonished. I married her because I hate her, he repeated to himself, and after thinking long and hard about how horrible it must be to be married to him, he felt an urge to laugh flood up to this throat, and he spewed out a guffaw. Clara couldn't hear him: she slept until they arrived at Urdinarraín.

IV

"Set everything up carefully, guys. We're staying here two weeks," the boss shouted, crossing the open field where the fair was being constructed. "Set it all up carefully!"

There were sighs of relief; there were protests. In one camp, those who wanted to rest; in the other, those who hated each new stop and wanted to leave as soon as possible.

Clara and Alejandro: indifferent. Two weeks in one place or another was all the same to them. The day before, their day off, they had had to work: to find a glazier, get the mirror cut to the exact dimensions, finish building the table. They'd hardly slept: when they could finally go to bed, Alejandro had left the light on, just like that.

The next morning, exhausted, she helped him set up the tent without the slightest enthusiasm. She was nauseated; her temples throbbed; she couldn't coordinate her movements.

In spite of everything, the tent looks very pretty, with those green and yellow stripes and the sign on top, Aztec Flower, in multicolored letters. I should be proud of it. Little by little, it's taking shape: first the tubular frame, then one canvas wall, and another, and the roof sticking out over the side, forming a canopy with a golden edging, like a fringe.

Her enthusiasm began to take shape as the tent grew, until at last she thought it complete and told herself that the other woman had been very silly to abandon such luxury to run off with a plumber. I'll never leave this tent, that's for sure, even if Alejandro yells at me and beats me to a pulp. She tried to banish her hatred and bitterness. Affection welled up in her in stages, affection toward that thing that was taking form and which in a certain sense was going to be her home.

Alejandro, on the other hand, didn't forget so easily. He chewed on his hatred like cud, nurturing it and reconfiguring it in all its possibilities. Occasionally he mumbled under his breath:

"Stop singing like an imbecile and get to work. Can't you see that this cord is too loose? You're good for nothing, nothing. You've got to be told everything…"

She let it all go in one ear and out the other, because at that moment a banner was being raised, or a backdrop curtain with its dazzling picture of jungle and flowers, a little faded, to be sure, but so realistic…

Shouts and cries echoed from all four corners, orders given by others. Clara would have liked to shout and sing, too, even clap her hands and run about, but Alejandro's furrowed brow stanched all her impulses. She saw the fat woman from the train passing by, laden with boards; she waved broadly and felt happy when the fat woman waved back. Then she decided to rest in the shade for a little while, and she walked about twenty paces to station herself by the nearest tree. She made a half turn like a soldier and couldn't repress a cry of wonder upon seeing that on either side of her lovely tent a metal and canvas city had sprung up, filled with colors and wheels and airplanes like the ones she had seen in Parque Retiro. She wanted to run between the tents, jump from one airplane to another, laugh and sing, but Alejandro called her to task.

She ran over to lay the matting on the rocky ground before Alejandro's voice could be drawn out in insults and reach the ears of the others.

Half an hour later, they returned to the hotel for lunch. Alejandro refused to accompany her to the dining room and locked himself in the room. Clara, alone and lost, found herself before the long table where everyone was gathered, and she wished she could make herself very small, so no one could see her. For that reason alone, every head turned in her direction, examining her with curiosity. Finally, the fat woman from the train motioned with her hand for Clara to sit beside her, and she seized that gesture like a life preserver.

"Thank you, ma'am, thank you."

"Just call me Chola, like everyone else does. Around here you have to be bold and just introduce yourself. So, tell me, do you like your tent?"

"Yes, it's very pretty," she replied, picking up her napkin without knowing whether or not to unfold it.

"You're right, it's not bad at all for a tent. But wear something light, because if you don't, you're going to roast in there."

And she turned her back on Clara to chat with her neighbor on the other side, completely forgetting about her for the rest of the meal.

Clara was disconcerted; she didn't know where to fix her gaze. Someone asked her for the salt, but she didn't hear him, thus losing a good opportunity to start a conversation.

When coffee was served, the boss, who was sitting at the head of the table, shouted: "At two-thirty sharp I want to see all of you in the plaza. We open at three. Anyone who arrives late is out of a job."

He stood up and walked alongside the table, talking to this one and that one; there were pats on the shoulder, reproaches. When he reached Clara, he asked her: "Didn't your husband come to lunch?"

"No, he's resting."

"Don't forget to tell him that at two-thirty he has to be in the plaza. And you – are you excited about your début?"

"Yes, very."

"So much the better." He favored her with a quick smile and disappeared.

At two-thirty, when they arrived at the plaza, a long line of young people was already waiting impatiently. Clara walked by with her forehead way up in the air before their envious glances, because now she belonged to the world on the other side of the ticket booth. Alejandro had grudgingly consented to wear his satin dragon jacket, and he looked even more handsome than usual. She wore a lightweight little dress as she'd been advised, and she had styled her hair as well as she could, with waves that fell over her shoulders, or more precisely, over the table.

Inside her tent was a bench, and on top of the bench stood her table. Alejandro helped her climb up, and he opened the two cover flaps so she could enter. She arranged herself as comfortably as possibly, with her knees against her chest, and he closed the flaps, which pressed lightly against her neck. The illusion was perfect; the line of demarcation in the middle of the lid wasn't even noticeable, and the mirrors, arranged in pairs at 45 degree angles, created the illusion of empty space between the four legs of the table. Alejandro let out a whistle of approval at his work and went out in search of the boss.

"Fantastic. Your living head is adorable." The boss pinched Clara's cheek, repeating, "Adorable."

Before he walked away, the boss said to him: "Here's your ticket book. Try to speak well and attract a lot of people. All right, get ready. The bell's rung already; they're going to open the doors."

Clara wanted to tell him that the ridge formed by the two rear mirrors was poking her in the back and could he please find her a board to lean on, but he had disappeared without even wishing her good luck. She also would have liked to call him over to give her a kiss, at least, but she could already hear the voices and shouts of the children approaching.

And suddenly, Alejandro's voice rose up above all the others like a storm, trapping his public. His voice grew deeper, then, and it became gentle, caressing, intoning words filled with seduction and promises. As he spoke, she forgot about her pain and recalled the night she had met him, so imposing on top of his pedestal. Now she was the one on the pedestal, or rather, her head was. Adorable, the boss had said to her, and she felt happy.

At that moment the curtains parted, and about ten people entered the tent silently. Alejandro turned on the lights, and the ten people uttered a single cry of astonishment. Please don't touch, Alejandro repeated, and the people walked around the bench, looking with a mixture of skepticism and awe. Clara smiled and stretched her neck languidly, while Alejandro explained that the decapitated woman was a secret, jealously guarded for millennia since the time of the Egyptian pharaohs, the same ones who had built pyramids and mummified their dead, but that the Aztecs had managed to discover the secret thanks to the magical sap of a plant that grows in only three places in the world. And he had inherited the magic formula from his father, who was a distant descendant of the great Quetzalcóatl.

Clara regarded him with the same bedazzled expression as the audience did, and she forgot to smile.

What he's saying can't be such a lie, after all; he has an Indian face with that aquiline nose and that dark skin of his. How could I not have noticed it before!

When he was done with his speech, Alejandro turned out the lights and made the people exit, taking precautions so that those who had remained outside couldn't peek. When the last spectator had disappeared, he approached Clara and whispered between clenched teeth:

"Smile! You've got to smile!"

She remembered to smile with the next group that entered because there were two boys who poked at her with a stick of cotton candy to see if that head could eat. Clara, who adored that sweet, spun sugar, would have bitten it gladly, but Alejandro kept the people at a distance, repeating: "Please don't touch; please don't touch," before beginning his pitch.

The public became sparser as the afternoon advanced, with only two or three people entering at a time. Clara felt drops of perspiration running down her forehead and filtering between her eyelashes, but she had her hands restrained and she couldn't dry herself off or even move, and when she closed her eyes, she saw a huge blackness as if she were about to faint. The air had become stifling inside the tent, and she wanted to speak to Alejandro, but he escaped whenever he could because he couldn't stand being enclosed.

After a long wait, a woman with children finally entered, and Clara deliberately didn't part her lips or even move.

"That head probably isn't very happy all loose like that, right, mommy?" the older boy asked.

When they left, Alejandro walked over to Clara and said furiously, clenching his teeth: "I told you – you've got to smile."

"Get me out of here for a minute. I'm so hot, and my back hurts, and I've got cramps in my legs. Take me out for a little while."

"Not even in your dreams. I've got people waiting outside. Don't you think I'm hot, too, in this damn jacket? You were the one who wanted to do this; now, just put up with it."

He turned around and left without even wiping the sweat that drenched her temples.

"All right," the boss said. "You people did a good day's work yesterday. If you earn just as much today, we'll be able to sign a contract."

It was Sunday, and they had three sessions. After much urging, Clara managed to get Alejandro to put a board in the box for her to lean against and to let her out when there were few customers. In addition, he got her a bucket with water, a straw, and a glass; at least this way she could wash her face, slake her thirst, and even take an aspirin if she needed one.

She was much calmer and more spirited than the day before. There was a bigger audience, and most of the people who came in to see her regarded her with awe and admiration. Whenever the gusts of heat seemed about to suffocate her, whenever some corner poked her in the hip, or whenever her legs grew numb, she thought about that red, red destiny she was fulfilling, conscientiously, meticulously, and her feeling of self-satisfaction revived. That day, Alejandro couldn't berate her at all, and at the end of the day, they signed a two year contract.

On Monday, a day when the circus was dark, silence invaded the hotel because the boss had loaded half the workers into his big truck to do some publicity in the neighboring towns. Those who remained behind tried to absorb that silence and take advantage of it. Alejandro was napping, and Clara had stretched out on top of the bed at his side, crossing her arms beneath her head so she could study the moisture stains that mottled the ceiling and try to discern familiar shapes in them, as people do with clouds. Looking for familiar shapes was a bad sign, she thought: she was sad.

That morning, she had gone out walking, driven by enthusiasm. Alejandro had just given her a portion of the money she had earned the day before, and she decided the best thing to do would be to buy him a wedding present, at last. So he'd see she was thinking of him, so he'd realize that she loved him, in spite of everything. She didn't know exactly what he might like: a nice belt, maybe, or a striped shirt. But Urdinarraín didn't have a men's haberdashery worthy of Alejandro, no chain stores, just a few individual shops and a gun shop. There's nothing worse than thinking about weapons, but in any event she stopped to look in the window, just in case ... and she discovered a folding razor blade with a mother-of-pearl handle, just like that one her father used... It seemed familiar to her; it was exactly what Alejandro needed.

She left the gun shop with the razor wrapped up in shiny paper and with a broad smile on her lips. She still had time until noon, and taking advantage of it, she decided to explore the city. It was just like every other town, with more people, true, but sprinkled with houses lining the dusty streets. So she wouldn't feel so alone, she pressed the razor tightly against her heart until, on turning a corner, two old ladies sitting in front of their house asked her pleasantly: "Going for a stroll, eh?" and Clara thought they had recognized her, and that everyone would accuse her of having tricked them. She spun around and ran towards the hotel. An Aztec Flower must never show her whole body...

Alejandro took the package without giving it any importance. "I don't need gifts," he told her, before untying the little ribbon. And then, when he saw the razor: "It's very pretty, but I won't be able to use it. I always cut my face with these old-fashioned contraptions."

Not a gesture of thanks, nothing. His displays of indifference, which she had admired so much before, were beginning to get on her nerves. She felt like she was surrounded by a solitude that stifled her breathing: Alejandro wide awake in bed turned out to be the same as when he was sleeping. The only difference was in his eyes, shining as he watch the thin thread of smoke from his cigarette float upwards and dissolve next to the moisture stains on the ceiling. Before, at least, she had been surrounded by men. Some were disgusting, true, but others knew how to make conversation and amuse her. Now, on the other hand, she had to give up everything except loneliness. She felt like she was suffocating, asphyxiated by loneliness.

A sudden inspiration let her recover her hopes. She sat down on the bed and, looking straight at him, said:

"Alejandro, we could stop taking precautions and have a baby." A baby to keep me company, she said to herself.

He kept on smoking, impassively, watching the smoke rise, as if he hadn't heard her.

"I want to have a baby," she insisted. "A baby."

He answered without looking at her, without taking the cigarette out of his mouth.

"You've just started working, and already you want to get out of your job, do you?"

"I'm not planning to quit my job; I just want to have a baby. It won't even get in your way, I promise."

"You don't plan to quit your job, huh? And what do you expect me to make for you, a pool table so you'll fit in there with your belly?"

Clara bit her lower lip. She had wanted so badly to use her head; now she couldn't expect to use her head, too. It was only natural. She began to wonder if that business of being the Aztec Flower could really be her destiny, or if she had been mistaken once again. She wanted to read her little red slip of paper, but she had burned it more than a month ago so she wouldn't be tempted any more. It was a pity; a situation like this justified everything.

The next day, they began at six in the evening, and although the temperature was pleasant under the tent, Clara felt worn out and couldn't make the slightest effort, despite Alejandro's taunts. Smile, smile, you miserable wretch. You have to smile, he spat out at her between threats, and all she could manage to do was grimace and think about the likelihood of her having a child.

Weeknights were empty and sad: sparse customers, sparse money, sparse happiness. For three nights, Clara could only form a grimace that lasted all the following morning, and into the afternoon, as well.

Thursday, at midnight, as they were returning to the hotel, Alejandro deigned to address her: "This business can't go on like that; we have fewer people all the time. We're going from bad to worse. And next weekend is going to be the last straw. We'll get the same people as before, and they've already seen you. Nobody pays twice to see the Aztec Flower; it's not like the ball-toss or the ferris wheel or something like that. Anyone who's seen you won't even think of coming back; we'll have to come up with something new. Think."

Clara didn't feel much like thinking, just forgetting, and she made an effort to fall asleep as soon as her head hit the pillow. But Alejandro didn't turn out the light, and he woke her two hours later.

"I've got it," he said, shaking her. "Now I know what we're going to do. Lucky you've got me, huh? *You're* not capable of coming up with anything good. Look, we're going to put your box outside instead of inside, and we'll make people pay to see how the trick works. It's a fantastic idea, get it? The same people who came before will pay again, out of curiosity. Then I'll roll you inside with the box, I'll collect the money as usual, and then we'll take off the mirrors so they can see. The ones who'll get screwed are the others who'll show up later on to show off their Aztec Flowers like they're the eighth wonder of the world..."

Still half asleep, Clara objected: "That would be like getting undressed in public. I don't want to."

"Oh? Now the lady is too modest? Has the lady forgotten she was a whore in her younger days? What the hell does it matter to you? Don't be a dope; don't go looking for excuses... now I'll have to find myself a table on wheels or something like that so I can put your box on top of it. Something strong, but easy to push inside the tent."

She was uncertain. Was she or wasn't she working with her head? And now that beast wanted everyone to see her as she really was, with a miserable body that she no longer wanted to show off, all bent over inside a box, with her legs spread apart by the angle of the mirrors.

Friday night they did their act as usual, but he had already arranged everything for the next day, with the same loving care a hangman uses to prepare the gallows. The boss had agreed, and he even wanted Clara to wear a white satin leotard, but she decided to be firm and refused outright. With the sequins left over from the jacket, she decorated a bouffant green skirt that would cover her legs.

The weekend could have turned out brilliantly. In truth, it was much better outside the tent, under the canopy roof, than inside, roasting in the heat. Besides, she could see all the excitement of the fair, all the colors and movement. She looked all around in amazement, and she saw the balloons and the little carriages going around in circles, crowded with children. It wasn't hard to smile at all now. She had an audience all around her, and many people were glad to pay to see how they had been fooled. Then Alejandro rolled her inside the tent and opened the flaps and removed one of the mirrors, and she emerged gracefully, asking those present to be kind enough not to mention anything they had seen in the secrecy of the tent once they went outside. It was so much fun to be able to speak to the audience as if she were an actress. She was almost sorry she hadn't accepted the leotard, but she came to her senses in time, remembering that her vocation was no longer what it once was.

It was precisely at the best moment that Sunday, when her happiness had reached its pinnacle, that Clara discovered the blonde. She stood at a distance, under a tree opposite the Aztec Flower's tent. She had been there for a while. Clara knew it, and she realized that the other woman had no intention of leaving. Alejandro rolled Clara inside on the table, and after the demonstration, he rolled her outside again, still enclosed in the box.

There was the blonde, always under the same tree, not budging, her long hair blowing in the breeze and her heavy breasts rising and falling as if she had run a long race.

Alejandro talked endlessly, without taking his eyes off her. As soon as he had sold enough tickets, he pushed Clara inside, almost against his will. The fourth time, when he had finished revealing the trick to the spectators, he helped Clara back into her box, but instead of pushing her outside as he should have, he exited hurriedly, leaving her imprisoned inside the tent. He came back for her almost immediately, but Clara had already arrived at the certain conclusion that she hated him. She had hated him many times before, yes, but never like this. It was something bigger than she was, something that weighed her down. Her hatred was so immense that she feared it might shatter the mirrors, and so she restrained herself, trying to calm down.

Alejandro, meanwhile, keep insisting: "Smile, you dumb broad; you've got to smile."

V

*M*onotony sounded like a train, like rain pounding against the windows. They had been traveling for several hours already, but Clara still couldn't get used to the idea that she would reach the sea at last. The previous day, Wednesday, at lunchtime, the boss had announced: "This is it, kids! Tomorrow we're heading for Mar del Plata."

"Big deal!" someone remarked. "First we choke on the heat in the provinces, and now that summer's over, they give us Mar del Plata so we can freeze to death. And the casinos are closed."

Clara, too, although she fought against her own skepticism, wanted to say big deal. For the last three nights, Alejandro had furtively gotten up and hadn't returned till morning. And Clara, accustomed as she was to living with men who weren't hers, didn't know how to reclaim what belonged to her. She watched him go and come back with her eyes half closed so that he'd think she was asleep. What a dirty trick! He was her legal husband, and he had no right to betray her like that; it was a vile, easy way to prevent her from having a baby. That's not going to stop me from having a baby with some other guy: I'll choose someone healthy and strong and good-looking for my own peace of mind. The bad part is that I signed a two-year contract to play the Aztec Flower and another contract to be faithful to Alejandro forever. It's too much for one woman to bear; I wish I hadn't known how to sign my name. I'm tied, hands and feet and head. As if this were my destiny, but it isn't, that's for sure. I'll fight till I burst so it won't be, so I can change everything one more time.

The train sliced through the plains, and the fine rain seemed to follow behind. The scenery was much greener, and there were more trees than anything Clara had seen from the window of a train until then, but the scenery no longer interested her. She didn't even care too much about going to the sea any more. Her head rested against the back of the wooden seat, and her eyes were half closed. Alejandro looked at her to see if she was sleeping, and she thought she hated him.

He was thinking the same thing, because the body of that blonde from Entre Ríos was lush and soft and deep, and in spite of everything, he had to leave her behind to wander around the world, saying: Ladies and gentlemen, I have the incomparable privilege of presenting the wonder of the ages, the mystery of the ancient Indians, which even in our own modern, technological age still astonishes and confounds us – and then open the curtain of the tent to reveal Clara's tired, worn-out head that couldn't even manage a smile.

The train pulled into the station, and they had to get off. Clara told herself she was close to the sea, and she breathed deeply to see if she could smell it, but they only thing she felt was the cold that got into her bones, and she had to bundle herself up in her thin wrap. She'd left the winter coat behind at Alejandro's place because she thought she wouldn't need it. She missed it: she'd been missing too many things lately, and she felt sort of abandoned. The black coat she wore had only two big buttons that came open every few steps because the buttonholes were too large; besides, the back of it was frayed, and the facing showed. She raised the collar with her left hand to protect her neck, and with her right she picked up her suitcase and started walking, behind Alejandro, to a new hotel.

When the meal was over, she asked her husband to go with her to see the sea.

"Forgot those crazy ideas of yours – can't you see it's night time and it's raining?"

She wanted to explain to him that the rain didn't matter, that she had dreamed of the sea for too many years to be put off now that she felt it so close by.

"If you don't want to go with me, I'll go by myself," she protested.

"For my part, you can go straight to hell by yourself. But afterwards, you're sure to catch a beauty of a cold, and you'll want me to blow your nose for you when you're in that box, sniveling. So, maybe you'd better just stay put. Get it?"

Clara meekly went up to the room, but as soon as Alejandro had left to go to the bathroom, she slipped away silently, running downstairs on tiptoe.

She ran for three or four blocks and discovered that the streets, dark and empty, seemed hostile to her. She had even forgotten what pavement was like, and her heels got caught in the cobblestones. At last she was overcome by the cold, and she had to stop beneath a street lamp to catch her breath. Nevertheless, she kept on walking straight ahead, trying to listen for the sound of the waves. At times she thought she heard footsteps in the distance, and she tried to move as quickly as possible: Alejandro might be following her to try to force her to return to that sordid hotel. Another sordid hotel. Like all the rest.

I can't run any more, and Alejandro is going to catch me, and my destiny will be to live locked up forever: inside the hotel, a tent, inside the tent, the box, and me stuck inside all of them, fenced in by boxes and tents and hotels, just because I signed.

Dark, lonely, cold. Dark, lonely, cold. Each step was a painful echo that repeated the litany. Rain had soaked her clothing and was running down her back. The only warmth came from her own tears, streaming abundantly and blocking her vision; even her own tears were conspiring against her. They grew cold, making frigid tracks down her cheeks.

Just then she stopped. It wasn't worth it to find the sea her state, not even able to appreciate it. Before she did anything else, she had to straighten out her situation, everything that was imprisoning her. Later she'd have time to see... To really view the sea, you have to come freely, like the sea itself, make it a part of you.

She lost her way going back to the hotel. She wandered through deserted, dimly-lit streets. By the time she finally saw the flickering sign, she was drenched and exhausted. But she had made a decision, and that decision kept her going.

Alejandro was sleeping in the room as if nothing had happened. Her hatred had grown, practically suffocating her: he hadn't even taken the trouble to go out looking for her, of asking her to come back. Just as well: this way she wouldn't feel the slightest remorse.

Her first impulse was to strike Alejandro with some heavy object during one of those attacks of rage that he himself had instilled in her. How contagious fury can be, even more than love or anguish or desire.

Her own reflection in the mirror seemed to look back at her with bitterness. She felt like breaking the mirror, just like that other one, to do away with all mirrors. But she clenched her fists tightly, digging her nails into her palms, and that slight pain helped her contain herself. That's wasn't what she had to do to free herself of him forever, to escape her terrible, itinerant imprisonment, that wooden box that squeezed her in on all four sides.

She tiptoed over to her suitcase and opened it. With exquisite care, she took out her nightgown, a little bed jacket, and a towel. She got undressed, dried her hair, put on the nightgown and the bed jacket;

now she could say she was ready. She found the razor at the bottom of her suitcase. She had kept it out of pity, in order not to leave it abandoned on the nightstand where Alejandro had discarded it. It wasn't exactly pity that inspired her to look for it now.

Alejandro, lying on the bed, didn't move. She looked at him closely, slowly, as if for the last time. Not even the tiny beam of light from the bed lamp, judiciously draped with a sheet of paper, or her movements, had awakened him.

With the razor hidden inside her sleeve like a card shark, Clara climbed into bed. She had decided to make a clean break: just blood, plenty of blood. And then, freedom.

She'd have to take a thousand precautions. First of all, no trembling. Gently she slipped the razor under her pillow, with an almost indiscernible movement of her hand... It had to be available when the right moment arrived, when Alejandro was most soundly asleep, when the light of dawn fell on the most delicate part of his throat, which moved with his breath. To slit his throat, just as she had slit the throats of sheep, back there in her village, without feeling repulsed.

Thank God the blade was so sharp. It could cut a single hair in thin air; it would cut through his veins by barely resting on his throat. It seemed too simple...

Later. There would be time to think about later. Everyone knew that Alejandro liked to sleep very late; they wouldn't come to look for him until lunchtime. Maybe if she asked them not to disturb him, they'd leave him there until the day when they had to set up the tents. And by then, she'd be far away. No contracts to get in her way, no signatures. Just freedom to find my own path. If she took all the documents, who would find her? As free as the sea. And meanwhile, just a tiny effort to stay calm. Calm...

She awoke because a stubborn sunbeam was warming her ear. In desperation, she discovered that it was full daylight, too late for anything. Her first thought was of the razor: she had to hide it. She reached under the pillow, but her hand couldn't find the slick contact of mother-of-pearl. Nothing. She groped farther, behind the bed. The razor wasn't where she had left it.

Her blood ran cold when she realized she was alone in the bed, that Alejandro had deserted his spot, leaving behind the hollow formed by his body.

She stuck her head under the pillow, trying to disappear, but his voice summoned her back to reality:

"Looking for this?"

She turned suddenly and saw him there, in the middle of the room, the open blade in his hand. He looked just like Asmodeus did when the cat was about to pounce, and her terror wouldn't allow her to anticipate the great magic trick which Alejandro was about to let her witness. Suddenly he became the Great Wizard, the first card in the Tarot deck, symbol of the living god who plays with life and death. He was the juggler, and he seemed to lick himself as he approached the Aztec Flower with ballet-like steps.

Clara saw the gleam in his eyes and realized the threat went far beyond her throat:

It's my destiny, after all. It's no use trying to escape it any more, or trying to scream or defend myself. I'm going to be the head without a body, without tricks or mirrors. And my head will sit on a real table, and Alejandro will walk underneath it with Asmodeus's black, hairy body.

Alejandro understood that at last he had her at his mercy, just as he should have done from the very beginning. Now she'll never slip between my fingers again...

But Clara bewilderingly raised her gaze, staring into his eyes:

"You have to smile," she said. "You have to smile."